SADDLE MOUNTAIN

**This Large Print Book carries the
Seal of Approval of N.A.V.H.**

SADDLE MOUNTAIN

Lauran Paine

CENTER POINT PUBLISHING
THORNDIKE, MAINE

This Center Point Large Print edition
is published in the year 2007 by arrangement with
Golden West Literary Agency.

Originally published in 1979 in Great Britain
under the pseudonym Kenneth Bedford.
Copyright © 2007 by Mona Paine in the U.S.

The text of this Large Print edition is unabridged. In other
aspects, this book may vary from the original edition.
Printed in the United States of America.
Set in 16-point Times New Roman type.

ISBN-10: 1-60285-043-7
ISBN-13: 978-1-60285-043-9

Library of Congress Cataloging-in-Publication Data

Paine, Lauran.
    Saddle Mountain / Lauran Paine.--Center Point large print ed.
    p. cm.
    ISBN-13: 978-1-60285-043-9 (lib. bdg. : alk. paper)
    1. Large type books. I. Title.

PS3566.A34S23 2007
813'.54--dc22

2007012704

1
LUNCEFORD AND TRUMBULL

Six days out and they were somewhere between Meridian and Spanish Wells with Meridian as their destination. They had seen just one other traveler in that length of time. He had been astride a leggy big bay thoroughbred and he had not come close at all, but had skirted wide around their solitary wagon, and even when Nathan had turned to ride out and make a rendezvous, the stranger had doggedly avoided even allowing Nat to get within rifle-range.

Smoke had said, "Outlaw," and had gone back to his worried study of all that emptiness, but Nathan hadn't been convinced the man on the thoroughbred bay horse had not been just someone who was scared out of their wits, so he'd said, "Outlaw, maybe. And maybe there's something on ahead that put the fear of gawd into him."

Smoke had no comment. For a simple fact they had been four days now passing through territory where normally at this time of year there were stages, other freight outfits, horseback and even buggy traffic coming and going. Not, it was true, as abundantly as the traffic back down between Spanish Wells and Albuquerque, or even on the road over near Tanque Verde, but enough traffic to keep people interested in one another.

For four days now they had encountered only that

man on the thoroughbred bay horse and he had been traveling in the opposite direction. Otherwise there was nothing but the far horizon, a few sheepy-clouds, and once a dust-raising band of mustangs in flight, to break the emptiness.

They were too far out to turn back, and they were too far from Meridian to make a dash for it. "Between a rock and a hard place," Smoke had laconically said, when Nat came jogging back to shake his head and look a little anxious. "It's not the weather. That's been perfect. And this isn't brush-fire country, is it?"

Nathan sat twisted in the saddle. "I'll tell you what it is, and by gawd we done the dumbest thing in our lives coming up here this time."

Smoke spat amber. "All right. What is it—and how was we to know?"

"There's tracks back yonder to the west, up along that low old bony ridge."

Smoke studied his partner's face. ". . . In'ians?"

"Yes. They was riding south and I'd guess the tracks are maybe a few hours old. Four, five hours old. Looked like a pretty fair bunch of them too."

"All bucks?"

Nat looked exasperatedly at his partner. "Now how the hell would I know that?" he demanded. "They were on horseback, not on foot."

Smoke did not answer. He clucked up the hitch and with Nat riding along beside the wagon Smoke made a wider sweep of the surrounding area with narrowed, tawny eyes. He was a lean, weathered, tobacco-chewing man with a touch of gray at each temple and tawny-tan eyes set in a bronzed, strong face. He was probably in his forties but it was difficult to tell. One thing could easily be ascertained, though: Charles—Smoke—Lunceford was solidly based in the things which ensured survival on the frontier. He looked scarred and wily and sagacious, and he also looked capable of handling the Colt around his middle and the Winchester leaning easily at his side upon the wagon-seat.

Nathan too, looked capable, but Nat was a half-head shorter, much thicker, and had pale blue eyes and sandy hair. No one would have mistaken them for brothers, but they had been partners for three years now, since pooling their rangeriders' wages and going into the cartage business.

It had been said of Nathan Trumbull that he could whip his weight and height in brown bears. He looked as though he had been compelled to prove it a time or two; there were scars over both eyes and his nose was thicker than it had originally been through the healed and rehealed bridge. He was a little younger than Smoke Lunceford. At least he did not have any gray hair, but otherwise it might actually be a toss-up. Not that anything as insignificant as age mattered at all. Particularly not today, their sixth one out of Spanish Wells when they finally saw another human being.

Nat raised a thick arm and Smoke nodded because he had already discerned the horseman sitting atop a land-swell as though he had been carved of stone up there.

He was distant enough to be out of rifle-range and even farther out of carbine and Colt range. He did not seem especially threatening. There was no Winchester held upright, butt-down upon his thigh the way most bloodyhands showed themselves in challenging defiance, and as nearly as Nat and Smoke could make out there was no coup-tassel to his war-bridle and no notched feather in his hair. He may have had braids but if so they were not encased in otter skin which was customary, too. If he had them they were probably looped up and tied in back.

"Scout," Smoke said, "and he's sure having himself a good long look. Likely he don't believe there'd be just one wagon."

"He'll soon know about that," stated Nat, slouching in the saddle. "Then . . . how much farther to the turn-off for Sam Tuttle's ranch?"

"Three miles, but hell, if we make it that far we'll likely make it all the way. If they don't jump us before Tuttle's turn-off I'd say they might not do it at all. Trouble with broncos off the Reservation is that you can't predict a blessed thing they'll do."

"I could sashay out there and see if he'll talk a little," stated Nathan.

Smoke did not answer, he leaned far out and craned rearwards, scanning that entire southward long landswell, then he grunted as he hauled back upon the wagon-seat. "Stay here," he mumbled. "That one's not going to talk. Look behind us."

There were two broncos riding along the ridge at a

slow walk. They were leading a riderless big leggy bay thoroughbred horse between them for the freighters to see.

Nathan swore. "Gawddamn! That feller—outlaw or not—would have done better to come down and go along with us. Three guns are better . . ."

"Arrers," stated Smoke, and expectorated. "That feller wasn't more than maybe couple miles back when they nailed him. If they'd used guns we'd have heard it. Waylaid him and used arrers." He looked at Nat. "We're safe for a while—out here in the middle of the plain on the stageroad. Unless they're liquored up I don't expect to see them come busting over that landswell. Not even against a single wagon. I know what those fellers write in the stories, but a sober In'ian's no more crazy than you or me." He looked at his partner. "Not until about sundown. We got until then to come up with something."

"With what?"

"Well, how about a cannon, or a mountain howitzer, or one of those Gatling guns?"

Nat fished for his makings, looped his reins and went to work manufacturing a smoke as he said, "I got a better idea. Wings." He lit up and grinned at Smoke Lunceford.

"We might get them at that," drawled the tan-eyed man on the wagon-seat. "Only later; *after*wards."

They looked around for those broncos leading that dead man's bay horse. They were gone westerly out of sight beyond the ridge. They had made their point.

"Odd no one mentioned In'ians being off their reservation," Nat mused as he looked out where that imitation carving was still sitting his horse watching them. "Maybe down at Spanish Wells no one knew." He inhaled, blew smoke in the direction of the scout, and shrugged powerful shoulders. "If those tracks I saw going south keep on long enough the folks at Spanish Wells will find out."

"Which reservation?" queried Smoke Lunceford. "Crow, Shoshoni, Blackfeet—hell, it could even be Northern Cheyennes or their cousins the Crazy Horse people from up north. And where is the army?"

Nat continued to study their solitary redskin a long way out, and if he listened to what Smoke had to say he offered no evidence of it when next he spoke.

"I got a feeling about that one, Smoke. He's not rigged out like a bronco. I can't see any paint nor any feathers, can you?"

Lunceford was critical. "From here? Of course not."

"I think I'll ride out a ways."

Smoke eyed the distant mounted man then shook his head. "Stay here. If he ain't bait to get someone to head over there I'll eat my hat."

The Indian moved, finally, he turned and rode slowly down off the landswell in the general direction of the empty stageroad, but northward a fair distance. Even so, he eventually got within rifle-range. Not carbine nor beltgun range but for all he knew those freighters in the battered old oaken wagon with their four-horse hitch of big brown mules had a rifle. Commonly freighters traveled that well armed. Carbines were fine for saddle-horsemen, but wagoners had the room for something much better.

Smoke, who was by nature a skeptical individual, had to make an honest admission. "I can't figure that one out. If he's baiting us he's taking one hell of a chance to do it."

Nathan, with a better view, finally, said, "No braids. No coup-loop to his war-bridle, and as near as I can see, no gun balanced across his lap."

Smoke, who had worked the east Texas ranges, said, *"Pukutsi . . . ?"*

Nathan did not commit himself about that except to say there was no way for these to be Comanches.

They kept the wagon rolling. Their mules were as unconcerned as they ordinarily were. They had a job to do, knew when the sun started down they could slack off, and that was about all they thought of between baits of grass and browse and drinks of branch-water.

When Smoke finally was able to make out the fork-off where a ranch had its brand burnt deeply into a half-stripped old juniper tree, he said, "I'm beginning to have thoughts about the Tuttles."

But there was no barefoot-horse sign up there, on the approach to the turn-off. Nat loped ahead, holding his Winchester across his lap and keeping a wary eye upon that solitary buck who was watching from farther up-country and a short distance from the roadbed.

He scouted for a short way then drew rein to await the arrival of the wagon. For a fact, there was no sign

11

up there of anyone, shod horses or unshod, using the roadway near the ranch cut-off, and as far along the Tuttle-road as he could see there were no tracks either.

When Smoke came on up and hauled down to a halt, the mules looked around with frank interest. They had never stopped here before, and that Indian up ahead watching meant less than nothing to them.

Smoke spat, looked all around and said, "I plain don't understand this. It gives me a bad feeling. They are out there, beyond that landswell sure as I'm sitting here, and they are broncos, and there's that solitary one up yonder without his carbine. It's wrong, Nat."

Trumbull pointed. "No sign going into the Tuttle place nor coming out. If they are truly on the warpath they attack isolated ranches every time." He dropped his arm and turned to squint out where that solitary buck was still sitting his patient-standing horse. "I got a notion to try and talk to him."

Smoke was just as skeptical as he had been before about that. "He won't stand, but even if he would, and a fight started you'd have all those hide-outs on the far side of the rim come boiling down on you. Let's just drive on over to the ranch."

Nathan turned without additional conversation to lead the way down the turn-off, but he kept watching that distant buck and without a doubt that Indian was as interested in them as they were in him.

Why he should be that intrigued, why he should deliberately sit out there watching, was a mystery, but then an awful lot that Indians did was a mystery.

If he were indeed a scout for the raiders out of sight beyond the rim, why didn't he raise the yell and bring down his tribesmen in a flurry of gunfire, because once those freighters reached the Tuttle ranchyard they would have plenty of support from the Tuttle ranch riders?

A half-hour later Nat loped ahead to a top-out in the roadway where he could see the ranch buildings on ahead. He turned and gestured encouragingly for Smoke. While he was doing this their solitary war-whoop turned and rode his horse slowly westerly back in the direction of his hidden tribesmen beyond the rim.

2
SAFETY—MAYBE

There were three riders and the rangeboss at the ranch, but both of the Tuttle brothers, Sam and McLean, had been over at Denver for the preceding ten days. The rangeboss, a whisker-stubbled, burly dark-eyed man named Rand Steenan, told Nat and Smoke that as far as he knew the Tuttles would not return for another week or two; they had an ailing sister over there, she was all the family they had left, and anyway, this time of the year the work had just about been all finished.

There were two youthful, sinewy rangeriders over in front of a big weathered log barn, watching, as Rand Steenan leaned upon a high front wagon-wheel to talk with Nat and Smoke. Neither of those riders knew the

13

freighters, and in fact Rand Steenan only knew them by sight, to wave to. Like most stockmen they got to know freight outfits by sight without ever really getting to know the freighters.

When Smoke said, "Did you know there are In'ians across the west ridge?" Rand Steenan nodded a trifle curtly. He knew, and in fact that was where the third rangerider was: southwest of the home-place on a good, fast horse, keeping an eye upon the countryside from a little butte down there.

Steenan fished in a shirt pocket, brought forth a highly polished oblong of brilliantly shiny steel. It was one of those pocket-size heliograph mirrors the army used. Steenan said, "He signaled you fellers turning in from the stageroad. Only, all he could say was that someone was coming, so that's why we was standing over there by the barn. We got rifles and carbines in there."

Smoke looped his lines and set the brake. "What's it all about?" he asked.

Steenan scratched his unshaven jaw before saying, "Mister, you know as much as we do. Yesterday we was on the foothill range across the stageroad and seen a hell of a band of riders—and their dust. We figured it was probably a soldier patrol but all the same we went into some trees on this side of the road, just in case . . . It was a hell of a band of Indians, feathered and daubed and armed to the gills. We come back home and been here since." Steenan gestured all around. "Why they bypassed us I'll likely never figure out.

Hell; what can you really figure out about those people, anyway?"

Nat asked if Rand Steenan or his men had noticed one particular Indian who did not seem to have a carbine and who sat his horse simply watching. Steenan shook his head. The only Indian they had seen close up, he related, had been a strongheart on a spotted-rump horse who came around the low hills to the east and scouted up the ranchyard but never got really close, and who afterwards had loped southward on an angle as though he intended to meet the main band over across the stageroad somewhere.

"Otherwise—nothing," stated Steenan. "We been waiting around here sweating bullets and haven't so much as heard one lousy yell."

He stepped back and gestured. "You fellers are plumb welcome to stay. Follow me round back and I'll show you which corral to use for the mules and where to park the wagon."

Those two cowboys in front of the barn watched but made no move to join their rangeboss. They evidently had been instructed to remain where they were, or else they decided on their own not to leave the front of the yard unguarded, but in any case when Nat and Smoke were peeling mules off the pole and stringing chain-harness upon the side-pegs of their wagon only Rand Steenan was out there to lend a helping hand, and as they worked they talked.

Smoke told of their trip up from Spanish Wells, Nathan related how at each night-camp they had sat around their supper fire perfectly at ease, and unsuspectingly silhouetted like a pair of greenhorns because they had no inkling there was trouble among the reservationed redskins.

Nat also said it made the hair along the back of his neck stand up to think of that now, because sure as hell they had been scouted up, especially over the last ten or fifteen hours when they had certainly been passing through a countryside emptied of other whiteskins who had known there were broncos on the war-trail.

Rand Steenan finished helping Smoke turn the big brown mules into the corral, and before going to the barn to fetch back a bait of feed he hooked a booted foot over a corral-stringer, let his gaze wander out and around, then back again as he said, "I'll tell you something: I been around 'em one way and another all my life, and I can't predict 'em or tell you why they do some of the things they do, any better'n the greenest settler." He hauled back to straighten up and turn towards the barn. "Give me a hand," he exclaimed, and as the three of them headed for the doorless rear barn opening that cowboy who had been keeping watch atop a low butte south of the yard came jogging in erect in his saddle and with his head constantly moving. It did not take personal knowledge of this man to appreciate how tense and "spooked" he was.

One of those two young men out front grunted and turned on his heel without a word to also enter the barn and to lead forth a saddled and bridled horse. He saw Nat, Smoke and his rangeboss watching, so as he spun the horse, then cheeking it as he mounted, he said, "Jasper's coming back. I'll take the next watch."

That was all; he rode out into the yard, drew the carbine from its boot and rode past the incoming cowboy with a curt nod holding his Winchester one-handed in his lap.

The rider named Jasper came across to the barn where the others were standing in solemn silence, and as he eased up to swing off he said, "You get my signal about them freighters turning in?" and Steenan confirmed this, then introduced Nat and Smoke as Jasper was loosening his billet and his latigo. He barely more than acknowledged the introduction with a nod. His face was stone-set and smoothed flat with something close to fear as he turned to face them, one arm draped around a saddlehorn.

"There's an In'ian out there. I didn't see him until these fellers turned down our trace, then there he was, sitting his horse like a statue or something, watching." Jasper put a steady gaze upon Smoke and Nat. "There isn't but that one, and he seemed to me to be interested in these fellers. He didn't make no attempt to run at me or nothing, he sat out there is all, just watching."

Rand was not altogether concerned about one lone redskin. "How about the others?" he asked, and Jasper shook out of his puzzled little reverie to lead his horse on down into the barn as he answered.

"They're on the west range as near as I can figure. Couple of 'em come over the rim leading a leggy big bay horse with a saddle on it. Then they turned and went out of sight beyond the ridge."

Nathan explained about the horseman, how he had tried to attract the man to the wagon and how the stranger avoided them only to evidently ride into a warwhoop ambush farther south.

Rand shook his head. "I got a hunnert questions and not a single lousy answer," he said, "except that the bastards jumped their reservation." He studied Jasper for a thoughtful moment before saying, "Your turn to cook?"

Jasper nodded, went off to finish caring for his saddle animal and to eventually cross the yard, still very erect, heading for the cookshack, which was off the east side of the main ranch house.

"Got a ramrod up his back," said the young cowboy who was still standing in the front barn opening.

Rand had an appropriate answer to that. "You will have too when it's your turn to go out and keep watch, and never know when one of those tomahawks is going to spring up out of the grass right there beside you." He turned to Nat and Smoke. "What you fellers hauling?"

"Some consigned stuff for the general store at Meridian, a few cases of rye whisky for the saloon up there, and some general freight," replied Smoke. "And a load of light goods for a cartage outfit that just started doing business up at Meridian. It's supposed to be hauled on over to Blythville. I think it's quilts and comforters and stuff like that. Takes up a lot of room but don't add much weight."

With that topic dispensed with Rand had another

18

question. "You know any Indians? I mean, you got a friend maybe among those stronghearts?"

Smoke scowled. "Sure we know some In'ians. Might even know that feller on the horse, except that I doubt it like hell because he won't let us get near him. Anyway, he don't have to be some redskin we know, he could just be one of their scouts."

"Why no gun and why was he shagging along and keeping a watch on you boys, instead of bringing over his crew to stake you out on the ground and carve on you a little?" asked the rangeboss.

Smoke had no answers. "All I know was that we saw him about two hours back, and after that every time we looked he was out there. You said it yourself—no one can predict those people."

Steenan accepted this and leaned to roll a smoke while he made another comment out of his experience with Indians. "There is something—if you fellers can't guess what it is, I sure can't because I haven't even seen him." Rand lit up, studied Nat and Smoke through thoughtfully narrowed eyes, then asked where they had spent last night, and after they had repeated what they had told him about that earlier, including a few more details, Rand Steenan simply hunched up wide shoulders and let them drop.

"Don't make a lick of sense, does it?"

Smoke and Nat agreed that it didn't, and they also agreed that if there was a reason why the reservation-jumpers had not attacked the ranch, especially after one of their scouts had looked it over and had certainly discerned that there were only four men to guard the place, that too had to remain a mystery for the time being.

What was uppermost in Rand Steenan's mind, with justification, was what the immediate future held. Anyone could have made a fairly accurate guess about what the ultimate conclusion of this outbreak would mean—the army would chase those break-outs back where they had come from, probably with some casualties on both sides, and probably with some court-martial hangings, and that would be that.

But would the stronghearts continue on southward the way Nathan Trumbull believed they would, basing his supposition on the way he had seen their unshod horse tracks heading earlier, or would they perhaps turn back and raid the Tuttle outfit along with some of the other isolated cow-outfits in the countryside below Meridian?

Rand was encouraged, and said so, by the addition of two more guns. Six armed men in a big stout log barn could put up a fierce fight and make it last. As he and the others strolled out front where they would be in position to catch heliograph signals, if any came, Rand said, "It's the night that worries me, and don't tell me they won't attack in the dark because of that old superstition that warriors killed in darkness spend all eternity stumblin' around in it. I know a darned sight better."

"Depends on the tribe," stated Smoke, "and the clan, and some other things. And we don't even know what kind of In'ians they are."

Rand would not even concede this much. He doggedly said, "If they figure the risk is worth taking they'll come down here with fire arrers tonight. Or they'll sneak in and set all the horses free and bottle us up in here on foot. Or . . ."

Jasper Jones whistled from the porch of the cookshack, and because the others assumed this meant a meal was ready they started ahead from the barn doorway. But Jasper was pointing westerly. The others had to walk almost to the center of the yard to see around there, down the south side of the big old barn.

That Indian was sitting out there upon a little rise in the land, studying the ranch and the yard, and now also the men standing in the yard looking back at him.

The rangerider who had been keeping the vigil out front said, "That son of a bitch is goin' to give me nightmares."

Rand Steenan answered in a growly voice. "If you are *lucky*, you'll only have nightmares. Do you fellers expect he's trying to make up his mind whether to lead his friends down here in the dark?"

Nat said, "No. That's not it. He didn't know me and Smoke was coming here and he's been watching us all afternoon. Maybe the whole darned day for all we know."

Jasper, having accomplished his purpose, turned without a word and marched back into the cookshack. The others remained in the center of the yard with a reddening afternoon sun for their companion, watching

21

that distant mounted Indian, and he in turn seemed equally as interested in remaining where he was, watching them.

Nat finally shook his head. "What in the hell does he think he's doing? By himself he don't scare anyone, so that's not it. If he thinks he knows Smoke or me why don't he just ride on down?"

"Naw," exclaimed Rand Steenan. "He dassn't do that. Not when he's part of a band of reservation-raiders." Steenan turned to glance out where his rangerider was also sitting astride a horse keeping watch. He sighed, handed the youthful rider at his side that oblong piece of polished steel and said, "Signal him to come on in. It'll be dusk directly. What we got to do now is get set for the night, and I got a bad feeling about things, once it gets dark."

Steenan led Nat and Smoke in the direction of the cookshack while the cowboy caught red sunlight upon his mirror and kept flashing it until the distant sentinel saw the message and turned down off his little butte heading for the yard. That solitary strongheart could have made a run and got between the rangeman and the yard. Instead, he continued to sit out there looking and not making a motion nor a movement.

3
SEVEN MEN!

Dusk came slowly and the quiet men in the Tuttle ranchyard lounged in silence outside the cookshack watching as their private, isolated world kept getting smaller and smaller as their visibility was increasingly limited. Finally, Smoke sauntered out back to the wagon and returned with two carbines. He handed one to his partner, and when one of the youthful rangemen asked what he had seen, he crookedly smiled and replied dryly.

"Four big strong brown mules eatin' and darkness a hundred yards beyond. Otherwise, not a sign of anything. Not even a *sound* of anything."

Rand Steenan sent the riders to fetch some food and canteens to the barn, and while this was being done he smoked, leaned upon the railing of the stair-steps leading to the cookshack porch, and sounded resigned as he said, "Seven years with Tuttle brothers and by gawd this is the first time I ever regretted not leaving this damned countryside."

"If it's going to get you," stated Nathan, "it's going to get you no matter where you are," and having made that pronouncement he looked in the direction of the big old log barn. "What's to keep 'em from shootin' fire arrers into the shakes on the roof?"

"Us," stated his partner very dryly.

They went over there, eventually, when the darkness

was as close as the edge of the ranchyard. Jasper Jones had shed his flour-sack apron and stepped up beside Nathan to offer a bottle, Nathan took a long swig, passed the bottle back and smiled in the gloom.

Jasper took the bottle to Smoke, then to Steenan, and finally to the other young rangemen in the darkness. When everyone had fortified their courage with a couple of swallows Jasper went into a tie-stall, dug down in the manger and placed the bottle gently under the hay.

He returned to the darkness where the others were standing and told the rangeboss he had to go out back for a minute, and would return. Rand made no comment. He was examining an old rolling-block rifle with a hexagonal barrel. He held the thing up to Smoke Lunceford. "They keep it hangin' over the fireplace at the main house. Mac Tuttle once told me it was the rifle they brought with 'em when they first came into this country behind a drive of shorthorns." Rand puckered up his face. "Far as I know it ain't been fired since those days. You care to try, if the warwhoops come?"

Smoke shook his head. He had a Winchester of his own with which he was completely familiar. When a man's life might be at stake was a hell of a poor time to experiment with someone's antique rolling-block rifle.

Jasper returned from out back looking as solemn as an undertaker. He walked past Nathan and Smoke without even glancing at them and halted in front of the rangeboss.

"They got an In'ian in their wagon."

Rand Steenan blinked at his rider. Beyond, in the slightly more distant darkness Smoke and Nat stared.

Steenan finally said, "What are you talkin' about?"

Jasper restated it. "There is an In'ian in the back of their wagon lying atop some bundles that are wrapped in burlap. I just seen him when I climbed up onto the rear wheel on the far side and looked in." Jasper, still with his back to Smoke and Nathan, started to turn. "Come with me and I'll show you," he told Steenan.

Rand faced the freighters and despite the poor visibility they had no difficulty in seeing his troubled and suspicious expression. Smoke shook his head. "There's no one inside the wagon. In'ian nor anyone else."

Jasper did not relent. "Herd them out there with us," he told Rand. "I don't know what they're up to but I don't figure to get killed over it. Make them come along."

Nathan swore, then turned to stalk out the rear of the barn. For a moment it seemed that Steenan might warn him not to go out there, but if this were indeed the rangeboss's intention he must have changed his mind at the last minute because although he watched Nathan he did not utter a sound.

Smoke then turned to also go out there, and finally Steenan growled for the two cowboys over in front of the tie-stalls to remain, to keep watch out front, then Steenan and Jasper also went out back.

It was true but they had to loosen all the chains of the

tailgate and lower the thing in order to have something for them all to stand on while they raised up as high as possible and peered atop the burlap bundle of quilts and comforters, where the Indian was lying.

He was covered with a soiled red blanket and looked dead. At least throughout all the racket of lowering the tailgate he had not moved, and under the high stars which were providing the only early-night illumination his body and his face looked inert and lifeless.

Smoke started to push aside other bundles to get at the man. Rand Steenan shoved back his hat with a thick thumb and simply stared. It was Jasper who said, "Why'n hell didn't you fellers tell us?"

Nathan turned on him. "How could we tell you when we didn't know it?"

Jasper looked highly doubtful of that. "If you fellers didn't let down the tailgate and boost him up there—if someone else done that—how the hell could you fellers not have heard the chains being let loose and the tailgate lowered?"

Nathan had no answer. Obviously something like this had happened, and yet neither he nor Smoke had known it. To stand there flat-footed and say he had heard nothing, had known nothing, would sound completely ridiculous. And yet it was the blessed truth.

He edged closer to where Smoke was straining to his full lanky height in order to get a better glimpse of the inert Indian. "I'll help you get him down out'n there," Nat said. "They got a lot of guts putting that bastard in our wagon."

Smoke eased back, frowning. He turned and saw the Tuttle-men eyeing him. With a little gesture he said, "It's the truth. We never set eyes on that tomahawk before. You can believe it or not." Smoke paused, considered the baffled faces around him, then also said, "But I think I understand about that other one—the feller on the horse who's been shaggin' us all day: *he* knew this one was in our wagon. Steenan, you said it yourself—why the hell would he be following us and keeping watch on us all the time, and never make an attempt to make war on us? There is your answer."

Jasper muttered, "A dead In'ian?"

Smoke turned. "He's not dead. Lend me a hand gettin' him down out of there."

They worked at lowering the Indian to the tailgate, while they got down upon the ground beside the tailgate, and in this position they could look more closely at the Indian.

He did not seem to be totally unconscious; that is, he seemed to float in and out of the darkness inside his head, but whether he knew from time to time that he was being roughly lowered from the wagon, or not, he certainly gave no indication of it. Even when Rand leaned and lifted away part of the old red blanket and probed with a rough hand, the Indian did not open his eyes, nor even flinch.

Smoke, Jasper and Nathan crowded in as close as possible when Rand said, "He's been shot. Looks like he's been shot twice, up alongside the head where that sticky hair is, and down here, low in the lights. Maybe

27

that lower shot is what puts the red foam around his nose on the upper lip."

Smoke shouldered in to make his own examination. When he finished he turned, glanced up where the Indian had been lying, shook his head and said, "Why did they put him in our rig?"

"Because they figured you was going on up to Meridian," stated Jasper in a very matter-of-fact tone of voice. "They know our medicine is a lot better than their medicine."

Nathan agreed with this. "Sure enough. And I'll tell you something else. That one who's been sitting his horse and watching us all day—they're partners or maybe kinsmen, and that one out yonder wants to be sure we take this here one to the doctor."

That too, seemed reasonable. At least none of the others disputed it, and after an interval of silence when Rand Steenan pulled back to wipe blood off his probing fingers, he said, "This buzzard just darned well might be what'll keep us alive through the night. Well, they must have snuck down and put him in the wagon at your camp last night, gents, and then all day today when they let you see them they could have come down on you in a swarm, couldn't they? But they didn't, eh?"

It seemed to fit together, all of it. Just one thing bothered Smoke Lunceford. It made his hair stand on end to think back to the previous night when he and Nat had been sleeping in their soogans beneath the big old wagon while those soundless black-eyed marauders had brought down their wounded bronco and without even stirring up the mules, got him placed high on the load in a soft place.

They could just as easily have slipped beneath the wagon with a pair of sharp fleshing knives and slit two throats.

Nathan and Jasper maneuvered around until they were in position to lift the Indian. The others came up to help. They carried him inside the barn and for all his better-than-average height he did not weigh very much.

Those youthful riders from up front came back, nonplussed, and simply stared. Finally one of them said, "Where was he—in the wagon, for a fact?"

No one answered. They put the Indian on the bed of an old sideless ranch rig which was parked close to the south wall, and where it was safe to do so, finally, they lit a lantern.

Rand Steenan's initial statement was true. By smoky yellow lantern glow they could see the wounds better. But they could also see a lot more. For example, their Indian was young, perhaps no more than twenty-five, and he was lean, brawny, and did not have either pigtails, nor braids looped in close. His hair was cut short, his features were finely made, and below the fringed hunting shirt he was wearing faded work trousers like any rangerider, a pair of scuffed cowhide boots instead of moccasins, and there was plenty of indication that he usually wore spurs on his booted feet.

But he had no weapons, not even a sheath-knife and

if he'd had anything in his pockets the men who had so cleverly deposited him in the back of the freight wagon must have taken it because there was not so much as a box of matches or a clasp-knife on him now.

"Damned if I understand it," Smoke muttered. "Who shot him—In'ians or someone else? Why us—if they was worrying about getting him medical attention why didn't they just take him on up to Meridian themselves; they wouldn't have had to enter town, they could have just laid him out in the center of the road where sure as hell someone would have taken him up."

"Or finished him off," muttered Jasper. "Rand; want me to fetch the medicine chest from the bunkhouse?"

Steenan had been making a closer examination while the others had been talking. Now he said, "He's not bleeding. My guess is that he hasn't been bleeding most of today. There's no way to know how much blood he lost, but he don't seem to have bled much on these burlap bundles in the wagon, so maybe he'd already quit bleeding when they put him atop the load." Steenan turned towards Jasper. "I don't want the medicine chest. I don't know what more to do for him that Mother Nature's already went and done for him. Thing is—how bad is that wound through the lights? It came out his back so the slug's not in there, but maybe he's got an infection or something. Best thing I know to do is leave him right here and keep an eye on him. If he starts running a fever or getting out of his head too much, well—then I reckon he'll die on us, won't he?"

Smoke dug out his plug and gnawed off a corner, then repocketed the plug and cheeked his cud while studying the Indian. Finally he said, "If he's been out like this since maybe yesterday, fellers, I'd guess he's got a cracked skull—a concussion—and if it's bad enough, he's going to die on us anyway. But," and now Smoke turned to look around in the baleful lamplight, "we dassn't let his partner out there know if he dies. Like we was talkin' about earlier, he's maybe all that's goin' to keep us from being hit tonight."

Jasper looked as though he might comment. Smoke held up a hand for silence. He had not said everything he'd had in mind yet.

"One other thing, gents: if they let our wagon pass today because they figured we'd deliver their tribesman up to the doctor in Meridian, they'd likely let us pull out of here in the morning and complete our drive up to Meridian."

This latter idea touched off additional discussion. For one thing Rand did not like the idea of losing the two freighters from his squad of defenders. For another thing, as Nathan pointed out to his partner, if that was an incorrect guess on Smoke's part and they struck boldly out on the Meridian stageroad again, only to be attacked, there was no way they could turn back and reach the safety of the ranchyard again.

Nathan was of the opinion that he and his partner had ought to remain right where they were. Smoke did not dispute this. He had not brought up the possibility of immunity from attack because he wanted to try and

31

reach Meridian, he had simply mentioned it because the idea occurred to him. He was trying to cover all aspects of this dilemma none of them had any experience about.

One of the young cowboys walked back up front and leaned to look out over the yard. There was nothing to be seen out in the darkness, but then there probably would not have been in any case; stalking night-raiders were just as zealous about not being seen as men like that youthful cowboy were zealous about trying to discern them.

In fact the yard, the surrounding darkness, and even the distant landforms which were ghostly in their bulkiness, were deeply hushed. This did not necessarily mean there was no one out there. It more often meant that there was no noise being made by nocturnal wildlife because there *was* someone out there.

Jasper went after the bottle he had so tenderly bedded in the manger and returned to suggest that Smoke or Rand pour some of the contents down their inert Indian. "If he can talk a little maybe he'll be able to give us some answers," Jasper said.

The others offered no rebuttal so Rand held up the Indian's badly lacerated head while Smoke got the bottle past the man's teeth and gently up-ended it. After four swallows Smoke removed the bottle.

The Indian did not seem to even breathe differently so Jasper said, "Pour in some more," but they did not do it. Rand let the man's head back down, gently, and looked concerned. "If it wasn't a busted skull he should at least have choked, or maybe coughed. Boys, I got a bad feeling about this warwhoop."

The others stood somberly eyeing the Indian, then they turned away one at a time to take up positions at both the front and rear of the barn, evidently willing to accept the judgment of the rangeboss.

4
NO CROW

They began their vigil as though all of them would remain awake throughout the night, but Nathan Trumbull went into one of the tie-stalls and fluffed some meadow hay for a pallet and within five minutes was snoring in there.

Smoke Lunceford stood with Rand Steenan near the rear barn entrance. Smoke was not bothered by something which seemed to plague his companions; since he chewed rather than smoked tobacco he had no trouble at all, but the others were all smokers and they fidgeted.

Steenan left a couple of times to go back and look at their Indian. The last time he returned after doing that he shook his head. "I never saw anyone take four or five swallows of whisky before and not show *something*. He's still alive over there, and he's breathing deep, but he might as well be dead."

Smoke said, "Give him time," then he reverted to a topic he had mentioned before, and about which he had recently been thinking. "If we're supposed to deliver that bronco to Meridian, Nat and me, they will likely be watching in the morning—at least that one will be watching who was keeping us in sight all day today—so suppose we *all* ride out of here?"

Steenan scowled in thought and said nothing, so Smoke spoke on. "If we don't drive out in the morning what's to stop them from thinking he died, or maybe that we killed him? They sure as hell will come charging in here loaded for bear. He's our protection; we'd be foolish not to use him to the hilt."

Steenan finally said, "Wait until morning."

Jasper came over to mention that he'd been in the loft to pitch feed down to some saddle animals in a north-side corral, and while he'd been up there he'd looked all around. He raised an arm. "There's a reflection of light off to the west beyond the far ridge." He dropped the arm and exchanged a long look with Rand before saying, "I couldn't tell whether it was far enough out to be the Anvil Ranch or not. Maybe it's just a big cooking-fire for the broncos."

Steenan was non-committal this time too. "Maybe. Go back up there, Jasper, and if you smoke don't set the hay afire. Keep watch."

The cowboy turned without another word. He had said very little to either of the freighters since discovering that Indian in their wagon. Despite the fact that everyone else seemed to accept Smoke's avowal of ignorance about that Indian, Jasper Jones remained aloof.

Nathan was still snoring an hour later when his partner went over and leaned on the stall-wall to look at him, then to shake his head and move away. How anyone could sleep like that with grisly death perhaps somewhere just beyond the log walls of the barn, was something Smoke Lunceford could not fathom, although he was not by nature an excitable individual and had faced his share of peril head-on. It was not that he was afraid so much as it was that when trouble arrived he wanted every sense alert and ready so that he could meet it head-on.

Jasper came to the overhead crawl-hole and poked his head through to hiss. Smoke was nearest so he went over to the floor of the loft-ladder. "What is it?"

"Sounds like horses moving real stealthily just north of the barn."

Steenan had come up in time to hear, so now he told Jasper to return to the loft-opening and keep watch, then he motioned for Smoke to go across the barn. "Wake your partner," he growled, turned, and lugging his carbine went over along the rear wall to find a safe place to peek out.

Nathan came awake without any effort and after yawning and vigorously scratching for a moment, got to his feet, picked up the Winchester he had been sleeping with, and with his free hand brushed off chaff as he listened to Smoke, then wordlessly walked out of the tie-stall looking left and right. He decided since the noise had come from the north and out back, it might be a ruse to mask movement in the front yard, so he went up there to find a hiding-place from which he could watch for movement.

Smoke went back where Rand was standing. The rangeboss shook his head. "Don't see nothin' and don't hear nothin'."

They stood a long while like that, motionless and without making a sound, but whatever Jasper had heard up in the loft must have come and gone because now when Steenan went back to the foot of the loft-ladder and hissed for the man up there, Jasper came over, peered down and said that regardless of what the others thought there *had* been horses walking out there, very quietly and very cautiously.

Smoke came over, tapped Steenan and said, "Where are your other riders?"

Without a word Rand Steenan went swiftly back and forth inside the barn. He did not find those two youthful rangemen. When he returned to where Smoke was standing the lanky freighter said, "How many horses was in that corral north of the barn?"

"Six," stated Steenan, understood what was on Smoke's mind, and the pair of them went along the rear wall to a stall, gingerly slid back a wooden window, and after a brief look Smoke pulled back saying, "Four head out there now."

Rand swore with feeling, but kept his voice low. Then he looked exasperatedly at Smoke to say, "What the hell makes them think they can get out of here alive?"

Smoke could think of at least two good reasons why those two fleeing cowboys might have thought that. One reason was because the moon was still not showing so it was plenty dark out there, and the second reason was that if the stronghearts were not keeping a surround in place out yonder, there was a very good possibility that they would not even hear the escaping riders. But what he told Rand Steenan was different. He said it laconically. "Daylight will tell the story. If they make it and reach Meridian we'd ought to have a posse heading this way tomorrow."

Steenan was not very hopeful. "You know the folks in Meridian very well? I do, and the number of 'em that would ride this far over a countryside full of rampagin' redskins you could count on the fingers of one hand. Anyway, those two darned idiots likely won't head for town, they'll head due east and keep going until they reach territory where folks never even heard of Meridian. And that, my friend, cuts us down a heap. You two fellers with me and Jasper."

A wolf sounded a long way off. The two men at the wooden window listened while drawing up very straight. The sound seemed to come from the northeast. Steenan began wagging his head. "Ain't been a wolf down here in five, six years. We been killing every one we could find ever since I been on the place, and before that the Tuttles been hunting them off the cow-ranges and even paying bounties."

Smoke hadn't thought for a moment a genuine wolf had made that sound. What he was trying to decide was whether that wolf-sounding redskin out there had been far enough to the east to perhaps be signalling the arrival in his area of a pair of range-riding horsemen.

The wolf did not sound again. Smoke turned and walked up front where his partner was, and out across the moonlighted yard where the yonder buildings cast gloomy dark shadows, there was nothing to be seen but clusters of high stars, none of them much larger than a diamond-chip.

Nat spoke gently from the interior darkness. "What's the commotion about?"

Smoke explained that those two young cowboys had stealthily left the barn with their outfits, had rigged out a pair of horses and had cautiously departed.

Nat was not very upset. "When they were here they didn't do anything but hang close together and mumble a lot . . . Is that what the wolf-call was about, you reckon; a redskin saw them?"

"Or heard them. Have you seen anything up here?"

"Nothing," replied Nathan. "Is that Indian dead yet?"

Smoke had temporarily forgot their injured war-whoop so now he turned to walk over along the south wall where that wagon stood. The Indian had moved. He was no longer on his back but was half twisted onto his side so that he was facing towards the barn's interior. The smell of whisky was powerful as Smoke leaned for a closer look in the sooty gloom.

A pair of jet-black narrowed eyes looked steadily back from behind down-growing black eyelashes. Smoke's grip on his carbine instinctively tightened as he said, "You're going to fool us all and hang on, eh?"

The Indian had almost none of that lilting accent when he said, "Who are you; what is this place?"

"This place is the inside of a log barn at the Tuttle ranch. Me, I'm named Smoke Lunceford. Now you answer a couple for me. Who shot you, and why?"

"Shot . . . ?"

"Friend, you got a hell of a ragged and gory-looking swelling up alongside your head and you got a bullet-hole through the chest—right through the lights from front to back."

The Indian exhaled a long breath. The odor of raw whisky was powerful enough to make Smoke blink a couple of times and to draw back just a little. But if the Indian had been about to speak, the sudden appearance of Rand Steenan, drawn over here by the sound of voices, seemed to work adversely because now the Indian closed his eyes.

Rand leaned for a close look, then turned. "Was that him talkin' to you?"

"Yeah. He didn't know where he was. He didn't know he'd been shot."

Rand looked long at the Indian, then laid a big work-roughened hand upon the Indian's shoulder and gently shook the man. Those narrowed very black eyes opened and fixed a steady stare upon Rand Steenan.

"You got a name?" asked the rangeboss. The Indian lay there without blinking, steadily staring at Steenan without opening his mouth. Smoke had seen them do this before. Rand removed his big hand and leaned a little. "Name? Your name? Where are you from? How many stronghearts are out there and what tribe do they belong to?"

Smoke could have predicted that Steenan would get no answer. That impassively dogged expression which accompanied that dead-level unwavering stare were symptoms of the mood Indians could go down into on a moment's notice and from which no amount of cajoling, threatening or promising could pull them back up out of, until they were good and ready to come out of it.

Steenan finally understood too. He turned towards Smoke. "Did he mention anything that might help us?"

"Nope. But I'll tell you one thing, he's no pidgin-English In'ian. He can sling the lingo as well as you or I can. You want me to make a guess about him?"

"Sure," retorted Steenan, looking bitterly at the Indian. "If he won't do it, you might as well have a shot at it."

"He wasn't with that band of reservation-jumpers. He's someone's rangerider. I don't know what happened, but I'd almost bet money on that much of his story."

Steenan looked down, scowling darkly. "How about it?" he asked, and got the same dead-level blank black stare as before, so he threw up his hands. "It's that damned gouge alongside his head."

Rand walked away up in the direction of the barn's front opening where Nathan was keeping watch. There was a slight chill in the air by this time; the night was steadily advancing along towards its darkest hours.

Smoke rolled and lit a cigarette, hid the flash of match-flame behind his hat and afterwards as he replaced the hat he indifferently said, "Redskin, if you know anything about those stronghearts out yonder it will likely help you as much as us if you open up a little."

The Indian answered without hesitation. "They are Crows from Burnt Timber which is a long way north and west of here. It's a big band. They are trying to reach a Shoshoni reservation over near the Nevada high desert country to make an alliance."

Smoke listened, eyed the wounded man, pulled on his cigarette and said, "A hell of a lot of good an alliance with the Diggers will do them. By now the army's sure enough on the way. Did they shoot you?"

The Indian looked up at Smoke through an interval of silence. He seemed to be making some kind of private assessment. Eventually he said, "I don't know who shot me. I didn't know anyone did."

"Did you know they had you with them, with the band as they came south, and that somehow or other they boosted you into my freight wagon?"

"No," stated the Indian. "I work for the Oak Cattle Company up at Staunton. I was out with the cattle and saw Indians painted for war coming out of a long line of foothills. I just sat there watching. I'd never seen that before. I'd heard of it at the mission school where I was raised, and I'd heard of break-outs, but I never knew very many Indians once I left the mission, so I just sat there staring at them. It was something worth looking at."

"Yeah," stated Smoke dryly, "and they shot you.

First law of survival with In'ians, my friend, is don't never get within rifle-range of them, no matter how friendly you figure they might be. Now tell me something else: who was with you when they shot you?"

"With me? No one. I was alone. I was sent out alone and the ranch was five or six miles from where I saw those Indians coming out of the trees along the foothills."

Smoke dropped his cigarette and stamped it to death. As he raised his head he said, "Did you talk to any of them, get friendly with any of them, happen to know any of them maybe from the same mission school?"

"I told you—until I came awake in this log barn and saw you, I didn't talk to no one. What town am I near?"

"Meridian."

The Indian's eyes widened a little. "Meridian? You know how far that is from Burnt Timber?"

"Yeah, I know. By trade I'm a freighter. I've hauled to just about every town in Colorado including both Meridian and Burnt Timber. Now listen to me—stop worrying about where you are—there is an Indian who's been keeping watch on our freight wagon all day. He knew you were in there as sure as I'm standing here. He's a strongheart; he's with that band of riders, but he don't do anything. He just rides along with us and keeps watch on the wagon. He can't be worried about me or my partner, and if he'd been scouting up mule-meat for the band he'd have brought them over onto us with a yell. It's got to be you he's interested in. You got any cousins or brothers among the Crows;

42

maybe some distant relatives that'd know you by sight maybe?"

The Indian stared at Smoke, waited until he had said it all, then made the only pronouncement which could definitely destroy Smoke's latest theory.

"I am a Cheyenne, not a Crow!"

The way he said it reaffirmed something else. Every tribe of upland Indians disliked the Crows. The reasons were varied and often none too clear, but the fact remained that of all the upland Indians the Crows with their high roaches and their hereditary non-alignment, were most disliked by all other upland tribesmen, so what Smoke had just inadvertently intimated had angered the wounded Indian enough for his eyes to flash and his voice to assume fresh strength when he denied being a Crow.

5
A MYSTERY SOLVED

Rand Steenan returned and stood beside the wagon unsmilingly gazing at the wounded Indian, and this time when he asked what the Indian was called he got an answer. It was terse and the Indian stared flintily at Steenan but at least he did not go back down into his stoic silence again.

"Douglas. Douglas McTavish."

Steenan recognized the hostility. Perhaps he was as baffled by it as Smoke Lunceford was. Eventually Steenan said, "Douglas, just answer me one question, and I'll give you a slug of whisky. Are those brave-ups out there going to hit this ranch?"

Smoke answered. "He don't know, Rand. He's a Cheyenne and they are Crows. All he knows is that he saw them coming out of some hills up by Burnt Timber, and the next thing he knew he was here in your barn. That's the size of it." Smoke looked down. "Tell him, Douglas."

"That is the truth," stated the Indian just as tersely as before. "I don't want your whisky either. I know how men like you debauched the Indians with your whisky!"

Rand Steenan stood there looking at Douglas. He seemed unable to think of what to say next. He turned on his heel and walked over to the foot of the loft-ladder.

Smoke was interested enough to say, "What you got against him? He's the rangeboss of this ranch and as far as I've ever heard he's a good man."

"He looks like a man up in my country who hates Indians and who knocked me senseless one time on the street in Burnt Timber—for no reason, I didn't even know him. Just because he hates Indians."

"Yeah but that feller's up at Burnt Timber, Douglas."

The Indian would not relent. "This man looked exactly like the other one. He's got to be bad too."

Smoke did not pursue this. He instead mentioned the medicinal values of an occasional shot of whisky and Douglas turned on him. "I learnt at the mission school how whisky debauches people. You know what that means?"

Smoke nodded his head although he was not sure he'd ever heard that word before. He'd be damned before he'd let a redskin know the redskin knew more English than Smoke did.

"Whisky is the evil of the world," stated Douglas. "It destroys the soul and rots the innards and turns the brain all pulpy. It ruins men and . . ."

"Hey, wait a minute," protested Smoke. "Don't get all worked up, you're a sick man. And besides, whisky has some good qualities." He smiled and turned to depart before the wounded man could start up his denunciations again but he did not move quickly enough.

"If you take three swallows you are debauched for ever," stated the Indian.

Smoke turned back. In the darkness their eyes met and held. Smoke said, "Whatever you say, Douglas. Now lie back down there and rest. If you don't think you're bad off raise a hand to the side of your head, and feel inside your shirt." This time Smoke did not slacken pace nor turn to look back until he got all the way up where his partner was. Nat was finishing a wide yawn and looked resignedly at Smoke as he said, "It's almost three o'clock in the morning. I'll lay you odds they won't come until just before dawn."

He was wrong. Dawn was only a little more than an hour away when he said that, and as his partner stepped to the barn doorway to peek out and around, Nat also said, "Rand Steenan said they are Crows. If that's so, how's come we didn't see any roaches?"

"Because they were too damned far away," muttered

Smoke, pulling back and half turning towards his partner. "And what difference does it make anyway? The only folks who worry what tribe a redskin belongs to is another redskin, to folks like us all you got to know is that they are In'ians, and whether they are out for friends or for trouble."

Smoke had a chew and remained up there with Nat until the eastern sky began to pale up a little, to be smeared its full visible length with flesh-colored pastels. And there was no sign of Indians.

Rand walked up from out back shaking his head. "A whole lousy night wasted," he grumbled and no one chose to point out the incongruity of Steenan's attitude now and his attitude last night. "Someone's got to go over to the cookshack and put the coffee on," he announced, leaning to look around the empty big ranchyard, then instead of stepping out there to cross the yard he turned and walked down to the base of the loft-ladder, grasped the uppermost cross-member and started up. It was so quiet at this hour of the very early morning that Nat and Smoke could hear every word the rangeboss exchanged with Jasper Jones up there in the hay. What it amounted to was that even with increased visibility and flawless eyesight Jasper had seen nothing—no Indians, no sign of those two cowboys who had tucked-tail and run for it, and no sign of anyone over on the north-south stageroad. It was, Jasper told his rangeboss, like being the only person left alive on earth, sitting up there in the hay entirely alone looking out the loft door.

Rand grunted about that, admonished Jasper to remain on watch up there, then Rand climbed back down and this time as he was ready to step forth into the yard he turned and said, "I told you—there's no way to predict what they'll do. Not ever."

Jasper called softly down through the crawl-hole opening. "I see one. I think it's that same one who was sittin' his horse out there yesterday afternoon. He's on a little rise almost due west, but you fellers got to look out the back door to see him."

They all three rushed back there, even Nathan who had abandoned his sentry vigil up front.

Jasper was correct. That Indian was out there, still with no carbine across his lap that they could see, anyway, and without braids showing, just sitting his horse watching the barn, the entire ranchyard, ignoring everything else even the greasy stand of rising black smoke far over westerly beyond the rims.

Nathan suddenly straightened up. Then he turned and hastened over where the wounded Indian was lying back with his eyes closed and his big chest rhythmically lifting and falling. Nathan took the man's boots off and returned with them. At the quizzical look he was getting he held the old boots aloft as he said, "I'm going to talk to him. By gawd if it's possible for us to haul up out of here I figure we'd ought to do it, otherwise we're going to be forted up in this damned barn for a hell of a long while, and I don't much care for that."

He winked at Smoke then stepped out into the

increasing, gray dawnlight and struck out briskly in the direction of the mounted Indian.

Smoke was doubtful. "He never could get close before, when he tried it a-horseback. You watch now; that In'ian will turn his horse directly and just keep walkin' it out of gun-range."

Smoke was wrong. The Indian watched Nathan striding towards him and sat as before, like a carving, for a long time, until he thought Nat might be getting close to sixgun-range, then the Indian turned and instead of riding away, he started walking his horse in a big, wary circle going out and around Nat until Trumbull had to halt and slowly turn to continue to face the Indian.

Smoke swore, then cupped his hands and yelled. "Stand still!" As Nathan heard and obeyed Smoke explained to the rangeboss at his side. "The Indian is trying to see completely around Nat. He wants to be plumb certain Nat doesn't have a carbine or some other sort of weapon strapped to him from behind."

Steenan said nothing and from the loft crawl-hole Jasper said, "I can't see any other redskins out there."

Smoke was pleased about that. He had not actually felt there might be any out there, or that the Indian was using himself as bait for someone to walk into an ambush. He had not acted that way the day before.

Finally Steenan grunted and said, "By gawd, he's riding towards your partner."

They watched without speaking or moving. The Indian came up to within fifty yards and halted, then as

Nathan strode a little closer the Indian swung off his horse on the far side. Smoke wagged his head. That was an almighty wary redskin.

Nathan raised the boots and said something which the men back at the barn could not distinguish. He walked a few yards closer, still holding aloft the boots and when he halted finally and lowered his arm he spoke again and this time the Indian answered. They very distantly and softly made out the Indian's retort.

Nathan stood easy and slouched as he seemed to be explaining something. The Indian, still with the body of his mount between himself and Nathan, leaned over the horse's back looking at Nathan and listening to him.

"Probably telling that one about the one we got in here," speculated Rand Steenan. "Where are the rest of them?"

Smoke turned to briefly consider that standing thick plume of oily dark smoke and said, "If you got a hankering to know, just climb on your horse and ride over the rim towards that smoke."

Steenan did not act as though he had even heard that.

Nathan and the Indian out yonder seemed to be getting down to a quiet discussion of some kind now. Although it was clear that they were still conversing they were doing it in such normal tones that the watchers back at the log barn could not hear a thing, then Nathan made a little hand-gesture and turned back, still carrying Douglas McTavish's run-over old boots.

Smoke and Rand riveted their attention upon the Indian. Now was the time to commit murder if it was going to be committed, when Nathan had his back turned and was returning towards the barn.

But the distant Indian did not move. He could have lifted out a sixgun easily enough and raised it across the back of his horse without anyone noticing anything until the very last moment, but he did not do this. He simply stood and leaned on the horse and watched Nathan striding away.

Steenan said, "Something awful strange about that damned warwhoop. He just don't act natural; don't act like one of them on the war-trail had ought to act."

Smoke chewed his cud, watched his partner eventually get beyond hand-gun range before expectorating, then he nodded agreement about that Indian out there not acting the way an Indian was supposed to act.

Jasper called from aloft. "Dust one hell of a long way north."

Rand accepted that. "Sure. It'll be the army. Two days too late, two hunnert miles too slow, and too few in the saddle to engage 'em. Want to bet?"

Smoke did not answer. He chewed, watched Nathan until his partner was close, then he shoved up off the barn wall and walked out to meet Nathan.

Rand Sheenan went out there too, but he carried his Winchester along and kept his head swinging from side to side.

Nathan paused, let the boots fall to the cold morning grass underfoot, and started to roll a cigarette while awaiting the arrival of his partner and his host, the rangeboss.

When they got out there he said, "Well; I got the darned mystery solved."

Rand said, "It's a long-lost cousin."

"Nope. It ain't even a strongheart. *It's a girl!*"

They stared at him until Smoke raised a hand to scratch his stubbled face and said, "Since when have Crows or any other warwhoops started taking girls on break-outs with them?"

"She ain't a Crow, she's a Sioux, and the Methodist brothers down at Ouray tried to give her to the Shoshonis when she was little and they wouldn't take her because they thought she was a Crow, so the Methodists give her to the Crows—who knew the difference, but who needed slaves, so they kept her. She's been with 'em ever since. She grew up with 'em."

Steenan dryly commented. "You sure got a way of gettin' things out of folks. That's all as interesting as hell. Now would you like to start talking sense? Where are those other devils and what'n hell she think she's doing shagging your wagon and all?"

Nathan pointed. "The main band kept on going last night. By now they could be southwest of Spanish Wells on their way over towards the Nevada high desert country. A few stronghearts raised hell at a ranch about six, eight miles west of here, and got run-off. There wasn't enough of them to do much more'n fire a barn and a hog-house . . . The girl talked them into fetching McTavish along. She then thought he was going to die so she got them to boost him into our wagon just like we figured—at night when we was asleep under the rig. She talked them into letting us go all the way up to Meridian so's McTavish would get decent medical attention."

Steenan craned out where the Indian was back astride, sitting like stone. "She told you all this?"

"Yeah. And some more. She thought McTavish was another Sioux. One of the Crows told her he thought McTavish was a Northern Cheyenne. She don't care. She grew up in a mission school too, sort of, and she . . ."

"Oh, for Chris'sake," grumbled Rand Steenan. "Here we are turnin' gray overnight and ready to go meet our Maker, and along with that, hungry as hell and in need of a shave and all—and you got to come back here now and tell us a story about some redskin maiden lookin' on a handsome bronco Cheyenne, and fallin' in love with him." Steenan started to turn back in the direction of the barn.

Nathan said, "I'm only trying to tell you what she told me. I didn't make none of this up. You better remember I was in that lousy barn too, last night, wishing I hadn't lost my rosary in a crap game down at Pueblo last winter."

Jasper whistled and leaned from the loft-opening up above to point. There were six or seven Indians riding one behind the other over along that distant low ridge across the stageroad. They were riding north and did not seem to be the least bit interested in the buildings down where the watchers were.

52

This brought Rand Steenan back around. He scowled and called up to Jasper. "Any more farther out that you can see?"

"No. Just that little bunch. They look tired and so do their horses." Jasper paused, then said, "I think that lady-In'an is goin' to ride over there to them."

But he was wrong, for although the Indian who had spoken to Nathan turned and faced in the direction of those distant silhouettes and seemed very interested in them, she did not heel out her horse but continued to simply sit there and watch, exactly as the men down nearer the log barn were doing. Then she turned, after the broncos had passed along, and urged her horse down in the direction of the barn.

She was well within rifle-range. Then she continued to approach until she was also within carbine-range. But evidently she could not force herself to come down into sixgun-range because she halted out there, swung off on the far side of her horse again, and stood watching the log barn.

Smoke said, "Hell; that's no good. She might just as well be down here with us. No one's likely to shoot her by mistake, then."

Steenan squinted at the distant girl. "Did you ever try to talk a squaw into doing something she didn't want to do? Did you ever try to catch one on foot? Just forget her; when she gets darned good and ready to do what she figures she's got to do, she'll do it. Until then forget her."

That sounded like sage advice so Nathan and Smoke followed the rangeboss back to the log barn.

6
A NEW DAY

Jasper reported that the cloud of dust he had seen earlier had diminished, and he also said that unless he was mistaken it was no longer coming down the stageroad but had angled off as though the riders who were making it had changed course, had decided to ride on a slanting southwesterly route.

Smoke guessed that the dust-raisers, soldiers or maybe possemen from up in the Meridian countryside, had knowledge that the Crows were going in that same southwesterly direction. In order to overtake them, or just to keep them in sight, the pursuers would have to ride the same direction.

Nathan and the rangeboss discussed coffee and Steenan went boldly out into the dawn-lighted yard on his way across to the cookshack. There was no incident, but as Smoke said to his partner, that Indian woman could see Steenan and she was armed. At least she had a beltgun.

But the Indian woman had never showed fight and she did not show any now. She was still out there, by the time the sunlight was beginning to distantly appear over the farthest curve of the world, and the bronco she was worried about was beginning to show more and more life as time passed. Evidently the splitting headache which usually accompanied the kind of head injury he had, had been blocked out by his long, inter-

mittent lapses between consciousness and uncon-
sciousness.

Whether that whisky had done him any good or not
it clearly had done him no harm, but after Smoke
explained to Nathan that the Indian was a confirmed
teetotaller, they decided never to tell him that he'd had
enough white lightning poured down him to make
most men half drunk at the very least, and on the empty
stomach the redskin doubtless had, fully drunk.

They went back where the Indian was and helped
him put his boots on. They also brought him a bucket
of water and some rags and helped him dilute and
soften the caked blood alongside his head.

The wound seemed to be healing well, and although
without any question that was always going to be a
scar, by combing his hair differently he could hide the
scar—if he chose to—but as a matter of custom most
Indians displayed scars out of manly pride.

The lung wound did not appear to pain the wounded
man, but then lung wounds rarely did cause physical
pain unless they were extensive. This wound seemed
to have been made by either a .25-.35 bullet or one
about that small, and while the hole in the back was
larger than the one in front, neither of them were still
bleeding. It was fair to assume that the internal wound
was not bleeding either because if it had been, that
Indian would have been dead—a victim of drowning
in his own blood—long ago.

Nathan was amused by the Indian's name but except
for a faint smile he did not betray himself. Indians

55

arrived at names by a number of processes and these frequently differed with the tribes. It was customary in the Colorado-Wyoming-Montana country for Indians to adopt the names of men they admired, and to pass these down to their children, and because Indians had never really been racists if they admired a white trapper or scout or hunter named McTavish, Douglas McTavish, their first male offspring would get that name.

But to Nathan Trumbull, whose mother's father had been a Scot with pale gray eyes, a ruddy complexion with reddish hair and beard, the comparison was too improbable not to be funny. But he was a discreet individual at times. This was one of those times, so as he and Smoke helped Douglas McTavish get his boots on Nat smiled perceptibly to himself but otherwise gave no indication he thought something was funny, and after the boots were on and he straightened up to face the Indian, the smile faded completely as he said, "You know a Sioux girl?"

Douglas frowned. "No. How would I know a Sioux girl?"

Nat was non-committal. "I don't know how you'd know one, Doug, but there's one out there." He then explained about the girl, how she had undoubtedly saved McTavish's life, how she had been hovering over him like a mother hen, and how she was now out beyond the log barn keeping her vigil.

McTavish stared at Nathan. As though he did not believe Nat he then turned and stared at Smoke, who dolorously inclined his head. "He's tellin' you the gospel truth. If you doubt it I'll help you walk over as far as the back doorway and you can see her out yonder."

Douglas did not act as though he wanted their help but he got it anyway, Nat on one side Smoke on the opposite side, and when they reached the rear barn opening Douglas leaned to stare over where the girl was still motionless on the far side of her horse. He frowned in puzzlement.

"I never saw her before. Why would she want to help me?"

"One redskin helpin' another redskin," said Smoke. "She taken a shine to you."

Douglas snorted about that. "We never met. I never saw her before in my life."

"You've seen her," stated Nathan. "While you was passing back and forth between here and somewhere else, you saw her. You just don't remember it. Anyway, whether you like it or not, she saved your bacon and you owe her, Douglas. You sure as hell owe her . . . And she's pretty, so you aren't coming out too bad." Nathan looked down. "Can you walk by yourself?"

He couldn't. He did not have to say so, Smoke said it for him. Then Smoke came up with an alternative suggestion for getting the pair of Indians together. "Nat and I'll leave the barn. We'll go over to the cookshack with Steenan. You can tell her we're gone and it's safe for her to come inside and talk with you." Smoke eased up on his arm-support of the injured rangerider. "Doug, she's a girl and she did a lot for you, took chances and all. The least you can do is act decent towards her."

Smoke stepped back and winked at his partner. They both left McTavish standing back there alone in the doorway. They had completely forgot about Jasper Jones up in the loft. When they got half-way across the yard, their destination the cookshack where smoke was rising from the overhead stovepipe, a faint and tantalising aroma of frying meat reached them and it was possible that if they had remembered the cowboy being in the hay-loft at this time they would not have turned back.

Rand Steenan was wearing his hat, his gun and belt, and had disdained wearing one of the flour-sack aprons which were upon a nail in the wall when he cooked. Nor did he act as though what he were doing could possibly have any importance. He was one of those rangemen who threw food at a stove and who afterwards then threw it upon plates to be eaten.

His coffee was black and strong. It also had a rousing good taste but that was probably an accident. He had made a fresh pot and he had used a different pan to boil it in, which may have contributed to the taste but whatever it was, when Nat commented Steenan looked suspiciously at him. He clearly had not expected honest flattery over anything he produced out of the cookshack.

Nat also said, "The In'ian feller and the girl are in the barn. She's too skittery so Smoke and me left them alone down there."

Steenan scowled. "Where's Jasper?"

He drew two blank looks. Until this moment neither of the freighters remembered Jasper being in the loft.

Steenan said, "It don't matter. He won't shoot them and if he's quiet up there they won't even know he's close by. Of course, he might miss breakfast." Steenan thought a moment, then spoke again as he turned back towards the stove. "Serve him right—he's never said a decent word about my cooking anyway."

Ten minutes later, with fresh cups of coffee, Smoke and Nat understood how it was that Jasper had never complimented the rangeboss on his cookshack capabilities. He could not cook. Could not even make toast without burning it and the breakfast steaks were nearly raw, the fried potatoes were soggy and corpse-coloured, and the grease they used to sop their toast in tasted as though it had been rendered from a gut-shot bear.

But Steenan ate it all with relish while the pair of freighters, who had not eaten in something close to twenty-four hours, pushed and scratched among the victuals on their plates then had to abandon even that pretense and go for their tobacco. That, at least, was palatable with more of the good coffee. It was a hell of a way to break a fast but if there was no alternative, why then it had to be good enough.

Steenan said, "If you boys still want to strike out for town, Jasper and I'll come along as outriders. No sense at all to him and me remainin' here if we're goin' to be the only ones. Not even if the main band has gone on, because there is still that little bunch of 'em we saw ridin' northward."

"That bunch will scatter like quail," surmised Smoke, "when they get up close enough to see that band of horsemen making the dust. I'd say you and Jasper will be safe enough right here."

Steenan did not argue, he simply said, "We'll ride along with you," and reached for the pan to refill his coffee cup.

Jasper came in stamping his feet and looking annoyed. "Thanks," he growled at the rangeboss. "Thanks all to hell for forgettin' I was up there."

Steenan made a weak little half-apologetic smile. "Well; it wasn't me as much as it was these fellers, Jasper."

Smoke blinked his astonishment but it was Nathan who came to the defense of him and his partner by indignantly saying, "What the hell do you mean by that, Steenan? He's not our cowboy, he works for you."

Smoke cut across the bristling words to ask what the Indians had been doing out there and Jasper, who had by this time become habituated to dislike both the freighters, answered curtly. "He don't know what to make of her and she ain't holding back with him. It's sort of like watching a couple of cub bears wearing boxing-gloves."

Steenan's practical nature asserted itself anew when he said. "There's grub on the stove and coffee in the pan, Jasper. I figure these fellers and I'd better go out back and start throwing harness on their mules. If we pull out directly we can make it up to Meridian before dark." He arose dragging a soiled sleeve across his mouth.

Nat was ready. So was Smoke. They were at least placated by tobacco and coffee. It would not prove an adequate substitute for a decent meal but for a few hours it would prevent their stomachs from bothering them, and right now as they walked out of the cook-shack, they were not thinking of food, they were thinking back to their long night of fear and dread inside the Tuttles' log barn, and they were also specu-lating on the road up ahead.

They did not enter the barn, they walked down the south side of it. Nor did they see either Douglas McTavish or the Sioux girl although her horse was drowsing in barn-shade where he had been tethered to a stud-ring, so without a doubt she was in there some-where.

The mules, blissfully ignorant of how close they had come to being steaks and roasts for Crow Indians, came forth in the warming new-day morning perfectly tractable and willing to be rigged out then backed onto each side of the pole.

Rand Steenan had finally abandoned his vestiges of wariness. He no longer cocked his head in an attitude of listening, and he abandoned the trait of swinging his head from side to side like an old boar-bear, scanning as much of the countryside as he could.

Even that greasy black smoke from miles off to the west was just about gone now. What smoke gusted upwards at infrequent intervals now, was more white than dark, so someone was evidently flinging water on the fire, and that, of course, meant that if there were a cowboy bucket-brigade at the far-away ranch where the barn and hog-house had been set afire, there had been no massacre.

Smoke even said he thought the whole darned affair had been overblown. Steenan looked at him with rueful expression. It was safe to minimize things now, in broad daylight with the reservation-jumpers gone. But Steenan said nothing, perhaps because Nat swore as the near hitch of mules refused to back up enough for Nat to loop the chain over the dog on the singletree. Steenan went over to lean his heft on the tug.

When they were ready Jasper came along with a gingham tablecloth wrapped around an assortment of food. He tossed it up for Nat to settle inside upon the load. Then Jasper looked around.

"Where's McTavish and his friend?" Jasper asked.

No one answered but the others also faced in the direction of the barn. Steenan walked over to the rear barn opening and stood, hands on hips, peering into the shadowy places where no sunshine ever reached.

Douglas McTavish came forth from the darkness taking slow, plodding steps as though he were very old. The girl, if she were there with him, hung back in the darkness. McTavish had a bandage around his head which none of the men who had shared the barn with him last night had put there, and there was also a bulge under his shirt where another bandage had been fixed into place.

Rand Steenan leaned to look around McTavish as he said, "We're ready to roll. As soon as Jasper and I saddle up a couple of horses. Will the girl ride along?"

McTavish shook his head, looked Rand squarely in the eye and said, "She is afraid to trust white men."

Steenan did not take that well. With a dour glance he straightened back from looking past. "They don't go raiding all over the darned countryside in the night like reservation-jumpers. Well; I'll lend you a hand over to the wagon."

McTavish stepped back, unwilling to accept assistance from Steenan. "I'll come," he said. "First, I'll talk to the girl."

Steenan turned impatiently and walked back to the wagon. He jerked his thumb in the direction of the barn. "She won't ride with us and he's talkin' to her now, then he'll be along." Steenan dropped his arm back to his side, scowled at Jasper and said, "Let's get saddled."

The girl came forth, kept her face averted, untied her horse, sprang up and reined off northward. Smoke and Nathan watched her go. Smoke shook his head. "She sure is spooky for a fact."

"Maybe she's got reason," Nat exclaimed. "Those pretty ones—well—sometimes they got reason enough to be scairt of us."

Douglas McTavish came to the door and leaned a moment watching the girl ride away, then he started towards the wagon in that same shuffling, old-man walk. No one offered to help him until he was beside the rig, then both Nathan and Smoke lent him a hand. Like most freight wagons, this one had high sides and no way to get over them except by way of the front wheel-hub, the driver's seat, and over the back of the seat down to the top of the load. When McTavish was settled up there he looked more ill than he had looked before. Clearly, regardless of how he felt about it, McTavish was in no shape to be ambulatory. Nat said something about this as he also climbed up.

When the mules were leaning into their collars Rand Steenan emerged from the barn leading his rigged-out saddle animal and a moment later Jasper also came forth. They got under way, the horsemen and the freighters, with the morning sunlight brightening a world which had only a few short hours earlier looked bleak as well as black.

7
AN EMPTY LAND

It was a magnificent day all the way across an emptied landscape. The dust they had seen earlier and which had veered away from the stageroad, was no longer visible. Neither was there any sign of those six or seven stronghearts they had seen riding northward in single file.

There were not even any cattle or loose horses to watch. Smoke got a fresh cud in his cheek and sat hunched and relaxed. Nathan rode beside the wagon as he usually did, while Jasper Jones and the rangeboss from the Tuttle outfit, also on horseback at the rear of the big old wagon, poked along also keeping watch.

But it was a lonely world they were passing through. Not that Smoke felt badly about being the only wagon-driver in sight. After what he had been through lately it would have suited him quite well if he did not see another living thing until they reached the outskirts of Meridian.

The wounded Indian was behind him lying flat out atop those burlap-wrapped bundles and while he did not look at all good, he had not looked much better since they had first discovered him. Of the Sioux girl who was McTavish's self-appointed protector there was not a sign, but knowing Indians helped Smoke appreciate that as elusive and shy as she was, they would not see her anyway, unless she chose for them to.

Steenan rode up beside the rig and said, "I'd give a heap to know where that little band of turn-backs is."

Smoke's euphoric mood was not going to allow anyone to cast a shadow over it. "Five miles west and riding like the wind," he told Steenan. "They was heading straight for that dust-cloud. Once they saw those possemen or whatever they were, believe me those redskins high-tailed it."

Steenan had a different disposition. Even under benign circumstances he feared the worst. "Those bastards could be hidin' in the tall grass on ahead a mile or two. You saw how elusive the main band was, and that was a hell of a lot more In'ians. Six or seven . . ."

Steenan turned and looked all around as though to lend visible evidence to his worded warning.

Smoke also looked around. He expected to see nothing and that is exactly what he saw—nothing—miles and miles of it in every direction. He leaned to expectorate before saying, "Hell; they didn't attack when they was strong and willing. Now, most of 'em aren't anywhere close and the others wouldn't run the risk."

Perhaps because he got no sympathy Rand Steenan dropped back to rejoin Jasper Jones, and Smoke smiled to himself. He was too confident they'd make it to Meridian without difficulty to even take Steenan seriously. When Nat came swinging in from one of his little scouts out and around, Smoke mentioned Steenan's anxiety. Nat too was unconcerned. There was just one thing that intrigued him: the girl. He was confident she was out there but he had seen no sign of her even though he had ridden farther than a scout normally got from his wagon in an effort to pick up at least some tracks where she'd paralleled them.

As for that little band of turn-backs, Nat shrugged indifferently. He was of the opinion, as was his partner, that they had seen the posse-riders by now and had scattered like quail.

Nat looped his reins to the tailgate-chain, climbed over the wagonside and settled up atop the load near the gingham tablecloth Jasper had flung up there. For some reason the cold food was much more palatable than Steenan's hot food had been. He passed over a handful to Smoke then leaned to rouse Douglas McTavish. The Indian looked up and even rolled onto his side, but he would not eat. However, he drank some water before sinking back into his torpor again, and Nat shrugged about that when Smoke looked at him. They had done all they could do, from now on in Nat's view it would be up to the Indian's constitution. Nat did not even believe hauling McTavish to the pill-roller at Meridian would make much difference but he did not tell this to anyone. His personal experience with medical practitioners had not been sufficiently salutary to inspire either respect for them in him, or to believe they were very different from the snake-oil peddlers whose elixir was at least sixty-five per cent alcohol, so their claims for its curative powers were justified to the extent that when they guaranteed that it made a man feel better, they were right.

Hard behind the wagon where the men from Tuttle ranch had been, Jasper called up for Nathan to toss down some food. He obliged by climbing over prone Douglas McTavish and leaning over the tailgate. He and Jasper Jones shared a restrained dislike for one another. Maybe on Nat's part it was more like disapproval than genuine dislike, but on the rangerider's side it was frank dislike and he'd made no secret of it since last night.

When he said, "Thanks," he also said, "Good thing for you fellers we was at the ranch yesterday."

Nat thought that over before replying to it. "We didn't need you, if that's what you're hinting at. Even though we didn't know we had McTavish in the back of the wagon, he was our passport. That's what the girl said."

Jasper handed part of the food to Steenan and did not face Nathan when he responded with a curt comment. "That damned squaw'd lie to her own mother. They all lie and most of them will lie when the truth would fit better."

Nat reddened and did not take his eyes off Jasper while he struggled to hold his temper. In the end he turned and crawled back up near the front of the load and set his broad back to the mounted men beyond the tailgate.

He said nothing of this interlude to Smoke. It was not important anyway, and Smoke was already perfectly aware Jones did not like either of them. Hell; they'd be in Meridian by evening and with just a little bit of luck Nat would never have to see Jasper again. Or Steenan, or even McTavish for that matter.

He finished eating, rolled a smoke, tipped down his hat to protect his eyes, and after lighting up he sat a little straighter scanning the countryside—and saw horsemen!

It was one of those sightings that make an observer's heart momentarily freeze in its dark place.

There looked to be about five of them but since they were clustered together out a ways to the northwest it was impossible to get an accurate count. He leaned and tapped Smoke's shoulder then pointed. Smoke leaned to expectorate, straightened back, eyed the distant motionless figures for a moment then said, "Not In'ians, so maybe they're from some outlying cow-outfit."

"They're sittin' awful still," stated Nat. "If they're rangemen why don't they just sashay on down here? We sure as hell aren't stronghearts. They never saw broncos herding a freight outfit."

Smoke drawled his next comment just as those distant horsemen broke up and started to move. "They'll be along. Likely they just saw us too, and they wanted to look a little first. That's natural . . . All the same, Nat, you better get down onto your horse and tell those fellers behind us."

Smoke kept smiling even after Nat had climbed down and had swung into his saddle. He was smiling even when he leaned to lift his carbine out of the boot underfoot and place it upright at his side.

He knew they were not Indians, but Indians weren't the only troublemakers by a darned sight. Smoke spat, craned around to look at McTavish, saw the Indian propping himself up as he too considered the slow-walking horsemen out yonder, and swung forward again as he said, "What do they look like to you, Douglas?"

"Maybe a posse," stated McTavish. "Maybe a riding crew. No trouble anyway." He then sat a little straighter and looked far off in all directions. Without mentioning it he was seeking some indication that the Sioux girl was out there. He seemed confident of this, and if anyone had a right to feel that way McTavish did.

Steenan suddenly broke away with Jasper Jones and struck out in a slow lope in the direction of the oncoming horsemen. Smoke thought it was an unnecessary thing to do since the strangers were approaching the road anyway, but when Nat came alongside to say, "You'd have thought it was their long-lost kinsmen," Smoke kept silent.

For a while, with the wagon making its slow and ponderous way up the stageroad, Steenan, Jasper Jones and those strangers sat out a mile or so talking. It was a lively palaver judging from the arm-waving. Smoke and Nathan watched without commenting, but from behind Smoke atop the burlap bundles McTavish said, "They are rangemen. I can make that much out about them. But I got a feeling they aren't plumb friendly."

Smoke continued to be silent. Nathan too had nothing to say now. Then Steenan and Jasper turned back to lead the others in the direction of the wagon, and whatever the attitude of the newcomers, there was no way to elude it for the men with the wagon.

The leader of those rangemen was a short, thick, bearded man with sunk-set pale gray eyes and a flat mouth. He looked capable of handling almost any situation he might find himself in. He was graying, which made him older than the younger riders accompanying him, and when Steenan introduced this barrel-shaped individual as "Mister Johnson Marley," the newcomer did not smile when he nodded towards both Smoke and Nat. Then Johnson Marley demonstrated the straightforwardness which was clearly so much a part of his nature when he said, "You got an In'ian on the wagon."

Nathan conceded that with a sulphurous look towards Steenan and Jones. "Yeah; these gents have no doubt told you all about him. How we found him and all."

The barrel-shaped cowman heard every word Nat said and did not heed one syllable of it. "We'll take him off your hands," he told Nathan.

Smoke stopped chewing. "Why would you fellers want to do that?" he asked. "We were going to take him to Meridian and hand him over to the sawbones up there. He's been hurt sort of bad."

Marley shifted his sunken, pale gray stare to Smoke Lunceford. "So we was told, Mister Lunceford. He give you a yarn about other red devils shooting him. I'm surprised you'd get roped in by a lie like that. There's been marauding In'ians wasting the whole blessed territory for days now. Some folks been lucky enough to see 'em coming first and put up a battle. Mostly, they committed massacres. This here one got shot sure as hell by some ranch-folk fighting him off. We'll take him off your hands."

The four rangeriders behind Johnson Marley were looking steadily at Smoke. Maybe they sensed his resistance to their leader and maybe they were just geared up for war, but whatever it was neither Smoke nor Nathan misjudged the looks on their faces.

Nathan looked with a bitterly accusing gaze at Jasper Jones and Steenan. Neither of them had ever liked

McTavish nor acted other than restrainedly hostile to him. And Jones, at least, had been the first to accuse the freighters of knowing all along that they'd had a wounded Indian in their wagon.

Smoke leaned to loop his lines around the upright brake-handle and to slowly remove his gloves as he studied the faces of the rangemen around the wagon. "The In'ian stays with us," he said quietly, his right hand resting upon the edge of the seat three inches from the upright Winchester. "If you got some special interest you can ride on into Meridian with us and take it up with the local lawman over there."

Steenan cleared his throat and began to look a little anxious. Maybe he had made a misjudgment; maybe he had told those rangeriders they could cow Smoke and Nathan. But if he did that, then he was not a very good judge of men, for after spending all last night with them under a theoretical siege, he should have been able to say now that they would not cave in just because some stirred-up cowmen wanted them to.

Marley sat his saddle with both hands atop the saddlehorn. He was out of it if it came to guns because he could not reach around swiftly enough. Several of the youthful, sun-bronzed cowboys with him were more nearly ready to fight. Two of them, in fact, had bare hands lying lightly atop gun-butts.

Jasper Jones said, "Lunceford, what difference does it make to you? And anyway Mister Marley's probably right about that warwhoop gettin' shot while ridin' with those reservation-jumpers. What the hell's the sense in gettin' all fired up over one mangy redskin?"

If it had come right down to it, that was not what Smoke had got roiled up about. Of course that was part of it, but what had stiffened his resolve was Marley coming up out of nowhere and giving Smoke an order. Demanding that Smoke and Nathan step aside and allow these rangeriders to drag McTavish down off the load.

He had no more illusion than any of the others had about what Marley intended to do: hang McTavish to the nearest tree. That too did not sit well with Smoke, who had known many Indian rangeriders who worked for big cow-outfits as equals to any other rangeriders. Whether McTavish had lied or not—and Smoke did not believe he had—it did not sit well with Smoke that these possemen or whatever they were, had in mind ganging up on a wounded, defenseless Indian, so he said, "If you fellers are so hell bent on catching your-self some redskins why don't you go manhunting down southwest of here where the main band went? I think you'll get all the In'ian-fightin' you want down there. And the odds would be better. This way—five of you against our In'ian, and he's sick and hurt."

Johnson Marley drummed atop his saddlehorn without taking his gaze off Smoke. Rand Steenan said, "For Chris'sake what's the sense in getting mad at each other when we got hostiles swarming all around."

There were no hostiles and hadn't been since the night before. Evidently Marley and his riders were also aware of this because one of the cowboys growled at Steenan.

"Nobody's mad, mister, we just figure to see justice done before they all get away. Commencin' with that one atop the load up there. Hey, tomahawk, what you got to say? You better climb down off there."

Nathan, who was built pretty much along the same lines as Johnson Marley looked past at the lean cowboy to say, "He stays up there, and if you knew anything about them you'd know he wasn't part of the raiding bunch. They are Crows. He's a Cheyenne."

The cowboy had been challenged so he immediately responded with a sneer and a loud-spoken comment. "Crow, Cheyenne, Sioux, Blackfeet, Shoshoni—mister, an In'ian is an In'ian, and when they take up the hatchet don't make a darn to me what kind they are when I see one. You understand that?"

Nat got red in the face. He was not a person with infinite patience. "Like my partner said, cowboy, if you want a redskin go hunt yourself up one from among those hostiles. This here one wasn't with that bunch, and they shot him to prove it. Mister, I'll give you some advice: stay up there atop your horse and ride along!"

Marley turned back to regard Nathan. He had been silent for some time now, evidently busy with some private thoughts. Smoke leaned to spray amber down the side of the wagon and to afterwards straighten up. As far as he was concerned, whatever came of all this he was already committed to one side and such was his nature that the longer this dispute went on the more confirmed he would become in his choice of sides.

8
A CLASH OF WILLS

Johnson Marley forced a false smile and made a little hand-gesture as he lifted his reins as though to depart. "It's not worth white men shootin' other white men over. One lousy In'ian." He threw a look towards Rand Steenan and Jasper Jones. "Nice talkin' to you boys." He turned to ride off and kept smiling all the while, his riders took their cue from him, also turning away.

Smoke straightened up with relief and Nathan slowly wagged his head with both hands coming to rest atop the saddlehorn.

Marley suddenly whirled his horse from a distance of about thirty yards and aimed a cocked Colt directly at Smoke Lunceford. Other guns appeared among his riders. They covered not just Nat and Smoke but also Jasper Jones and Rand Steenan.

"Throw down your guns," called Marley in a cold tone. "Throw them down and don't make a bad move. I'd as leave hang In'ian lovers as In'ians. *Throw them down, all of you!*"

Steenan swore and lifted out his Colt to let it fall. At his side Jasper did the same but without any profanity. Jasper kept staring at Johnson Marley. He seemed unable to decide whether to be furious at being duped or satisfied that Marley was going to hang the Indian after all.

Smoke sighed, leaned to pitch the carbine over the

side, and as he did this he said, "Do like he says, Nat. Throw them down."

There was no choice unless Nathan were tired of this life, and he knew it, so he disarmed himself, red as a beet in the face. He turned from Marley to glare at Jasper Jones. "You son of a bitch," he said in a soft tone.

Jasper did not have an opportunity to reply. Marley gave Smoke another order as he and his crew rode back a few yards. "Toss that mangy redskin down off the load!"

Smoke's answer was blunt. "I'll be damned if I'll do that."

He and Marley exchanged a long look then the cowman began tilting his weapon a little in Smoke's direction, and behind the wagon-seat Douglas McTavish said, "Lend me a hand, Mister Lunceford."

He got over onto the high seat unaided but he was not in fit shape to swing out over and climb down the side of the wagon. Nathan edged his horse closer and leaned to offer an arm. It was that, or watch them shoot the Indian up there on the seat, beside his partner. But Nat's high color lingered and his lips were sucked flat. However this affair ended one thing was clear enough; those rangemen had made an implacable enemy out of Nathan Trumbull. Smoke could have told them that; he knew how blind-stubborn his partner became over something like this. Any kind of total injustice.

As he leaned far down to keep a grip on McTavish to the very ground beside the wagon, Nat said, "Don't help them, Douglas. Don't cooperate with the bastards." Then Nat hauled back upright in his saddle with the unsteady, wounded Indian standing close enough to place an outstretched hand upon Nat's horse to steady himself.

"I'll tell you for the last time," Nathan said to Johnson Marley. "He's not a Crow. He had nothing to do with those break-outs."

Marley had already demonstrated that he only heard what he chose to hear. He was staring icily at Douglas McTavish, his cocked Colt tipped carelessly downward in the same direction. "Walk," he commanded. "Walk west from here, don't stop and don't turn around."

McTavish was weak and he was unsteady, but he drew himself up with pathetic pride and hesitated a moment before starting away. It was clear to them all that he would be unable to walk very far, and that sharp-faced cowboy who had challenged Nathan earlier, now carelessly aimed his sixgun and said, "Why waste time, Johnson, why not kill the black bastard right here and get it over with."

Marley's reply was ambiguous enough to reveal a little more about how Johnson Marley thought. "I'm tempted to do that, but since he walks up on his hind legs like the rest of us, and wears britches, he's entitled to a tailgate-trial."

One of the other cowboys, perhaps emboldened by his companion's outspokenness, said, "Then instead of hauling him couple miles back where we seen the last tree, Mister Marley, let's just take off the mules and hoist the tongue of the wagon and hang him to that. Otherwise we're going to be late gettin' away from here."

Rand Steenan finally had been driven into a position where he had to take a stand, and while he had favored the stockmen up until now, when they were clearly going to kill McTavish, something was rebelling inside him so he said, "Mister Marley; you said out yonder when we first talked you was of a mind to haul him to Meridian for the law to handle."

Marley did not argue, he simply said, "It'll take too long and we still got to ride south today before nightfall and see if we can't catch a few more of the killin', stealin', mangy bastards."

A cowboy leaned and glared at Douglas McTavish. "Walk!" he commanded. "Otherwise I'm going to drop a rope round your neck and drag you at a run. Now walk, you worthless son of a bitch!"

McTavish looked around at Nathan and Smoke. They gazed steadily back, and although the Indian really had no particular reason up until now to feel especially friendly towards either of them, he smiled, then he turned to start walking.

Nat and Smoke sat like stone, watching. When McTavish shuffled past that leaning cowboy, the one who had said he'd drag McTavish at the end of his lariat, the rider's cruel eyes narrowed in an even stronger look of hatred and he raised his sixgun for an overhand strike.

Nathan erupted. "You yellow bastard! You hit him and I'll pull you off that horse and stomp the wadding out of you!"

Maybe Nathan's abrupt ferocity shocked or stunned the cowboy but at any rate he did not allow the sixgun to descend until McTavish was past, then he slowly lowered it, his face white to the hat-brim as he fixedly stared at Nathan Trumbull. He clearly was an individual to whom any kind of fight-talk would bring the predictable response. But there were eight witnesses so he dared not pull the trigger on Nat in cold blood.

McTavish had just about reached the limit of his strength. He paused, leaned to rest a hand upon the shoulder of one of the other rangemen's horse, and this time the cowboy offered no antagonism.

Marley was watching the enraged rangerider. He did not seem inclined to prevent him from committing murder. Maybe he was hoping it would happen, but Rand Steenan wasn't and he said, "Hold up, mister. Don't let no one bait you into something like plain murder."

The cowboy turned on Steenan. "You—you and your big talk out yonder about these fellers havin' a tomahawk along and wantin' to see justice done and all!"

Steenan steadfastly refused to look in the direction of the wagon where Nathan and Smoke were staring at him. He reddened a little though, so he was not impervious to the silent thoughts of the freighters. He jutted his jaw in the direction of McTavish. "Let the law have him. Let the law settle it. Otherwise you fellers are going to be in trouble up to your hocks. Let the law at Meridian . . ."

"Oh, shut up," snarled the angered rangerider, and swung back towards Nathan.

McTavish's knees sprang outward and he slowly fell to the ground. The horse beside him softly snorted and side-passed, then arched its neck and gazed sidelong at the prone Indian.

No one said a word but that angry cowboy took down his lariat and with his eyes upon the downed Indian began shaking out a small loop. His intention was clear enough. He had said he would drag McTavish to death behind his speeding horse or words to that effect, and he had been furious enough to say them so loudly that all the other men had heard him.

He backed his horse around with his left hand and held the little bear-cat loop poised in the other hand. But roping a man standing upright was different than trying to rope a man who was flat out on the ground. There was nothing much to slide the loop over, on the ground.

The cowboy said, "Hey, warwhoop—look up here."

McTavish weakly fumbled along the ground as though trying very hard to obey. Nat called over. "Stay down, Douglas. Keep flat down!"

That angry rangerider suddenly turned on Nathan and would have made a cast except that Nat reacted by instinct and leaned his upper body against the wagon-side so there was no way for the loop to catch him.

The cowboy jumped off his horse and grabbed

McTavish by the hair, wrenched him part way up off the ground and settled the rope into place around the Indian's throat, then he turned and sprang astride.

A solitary gunshot rang out. No one moved for two seconds, until the cowboy who had been in the process of getting settled over leather and who had been ready to take two dallies, slowly raised up to his full height in the saddle, turned and showed an expression of total astonishment, then he dropped the rope, leaned, kept right on leaning until he was over-balanced, and slid to the ground.

Smoke and Nathan did not wait. They had no more idea of what had happened than any of the other men, but they knew one thing for a fact. This was the only chance they were going to get, and it was not a very good chance, either.

Nathan dived off his horse and rolled in the roadway dirt to come half up off the ground cocking the Colt he had been forced to jettison. Johnson Marley fired, as did one of the other cowboys. They both missed.

Smoke turned and dived off the high seat upon the opposite side of the wagon. He hit the ground hard and rolled beneath the wagon just as Nat fired point-blank at Johnson Marley. The cowman acted as though he had been hit high in the body by someone swinging a heavy sledge. His entire upper torso bent back, his hat flew and his feet came out of the stirrups as he continued on over backwards until he fell over the rump of his startled horse.

Rand Steenan was yelling for them to stop but Jasper

Jones was already on the ground using his horse as a body-shield while he looked left and right for the gun he had been forced to throw away.

Someone from out back fired again. It was the same weapon which had shot the first rangerider off his horse and until Smoke could make certain of that soiled puff of distant gunsmoke from below the mounted men in front of him, he had no idea who had started this fight.

It was someone back about thirty yards in the tall grass to the west of the stageroad: the identity hit Smoke like a blow. *The Sioux girl!*

Finally the rangeriders with Johnson Marley sensed that they were under an alien attack and they twisted to try and locate the enemy. That far-off gunsmoke was still hanging above the grass but the girl had rolled away by then. One cowboy jumped off his horse and hit the ground yelling that they were surrounded. That may have been the reason his companions also unloaded. Freed horses turned and fled. Nat's horse fled with the other animals.

Smoke yelled at Jasper Jones to hold his animal and although the horse tried to lunge free Jasper did indeed cling to him.

The fight was over. It had only lasted perhaps forty seconds. Perhaps not even that long but there were two dead men lying in the roadway, that vile-tempered rangerider, and Johnson Marley. The rangerider had been shot in the back. Marley had taken the full power of Nat's forty-four slug through the brisket and he had been dead before he had completed that backward flip.

Smoke had a cocked Winchester in both hands aiming on a ground-sluicing angle directly where those exposed, horseless rangemen were lying. "Oh, you sons of bitches," he sang out. "I wish to hell I had a sawed off shotgun, I'd splatter you over the prairie! Throw away your guns and stand up!"

For a long moment there was nothing in the way of movement. No one even spoke, then Douglas McTavish sat up and looked at the man on his right, the man whose horse McTavish had been steadying himself upon when he'd collapsed. Douglas leaned and gently took the rider's Colt right out of the man's slack fingers. Then he turned to point the gun at another rangeman. They began throwing aside their weapons.

Nat walked stiffly to the dead cowboy, toed him over, stared, then toed him face-down and stepped over to Johnson Marley. When he was satisfied he straightened up and peered far out. There was no longer any of that whitish-gray burnt powder out there. He took down a big breath and slowly expelled it, turned toward McTavish and said, "I'd plumb forgot about her. You know what I think? She may be shy and all, but she's sure as hell one mighty powerful warrior-lady."

Smoke crawled from beneath the wagon and gestured southward as he eased off the hammer of his Winchester. "Jasper, ride down those blasted horses and fetch them back here. And mister, if you get any silly notion about not coming back, take my word for it that since I'm not overly fond of you anyway, if you double-cross us now I'll hunt you down if it takes me ten years."

Jasper mounted, still unarmed, and turned to jog stiffly southward after the loose stock.

9
THE ROAD NORTH

Steenan came forward to help disarm and herd the captive rangeriders and Nathan swore at him. "You miserable turn-coat bastard. By my lights you'd ought to be over there beside Marley!"

Steenan had taken all the cursing he was going to take. He jumped at Nathan with a snarl, swung with his right fist and hit air because Nathan was under the swinging arm. He came up inside Steenan's guard and Nathan had the shoulders and arms of a bear. He sank one fist wrist-deep into Steenan's middle, aimed higher and as Steenan doubled over Nat caught him on the slant of the jaw with the other fist. Blood flew, Steenan went awkwardly turning sideways, and fell hard.

Smoke looked annoyed but kept silent. The disarmed rangemen stood watching, being careful not to even show on their faces that they did not approve of Nathan.

There were three rangeriders, and after Nathan had growled for them to congregate by the side of the wagon, he went around gathering up weapons which he took over to the wagon and flung over the side, Nathan was still in a vile mood.

Smoke went over to lend the Indian a hand back to the wagon where he eased him down with a hard grin and said, "For a sick feller you sure been gettin' your share of exercise lately." He looked around. "How about her? Will she come in if I call?"

McTavish did not believe the girl would come in even if *he* called her and said so. Then he shifted his attention from Smoke out over the empty landscape beyond. "She shot the one who was going to drag me?"

Smoke confirmed it curtly. "Neat as a whistle, from back to front. And that was a hell of a shot from someone with only a sixgun."

"I'd ought to go out there to her," murmured McTavish, and Smoke said, "Sure—how?" and that ended it. McTavish could not begin to walk out that far.

Nathan had his captives thoroughly cowed. It helped that the Tuttle ranch rangeboss was bleeding in the dirt of the roadway, his mouth smashed. It also helped that the man who had led them, Johnson Marley, was dead.

When Nathan asked them about Marley they did not hold back a thing. He owned a ranch east of the stageroad and slightly southward, and when he'd heard there were stronghearts in the area he brought his riding crew over closer to the stageroad. His idea, they told Nathan, had been to make a run northward to the safety of Meridian. Then they made a big scout and discovered that most of the Indians had already departed on their southwesterly trip and Marley told his riders they might as well try to find a stray bronco or two and hang them on their way to town. They had seen the freight wagon with its outriders and without any idea that there might be an Indian down there, had decided to watch and make certain it was safe to do so before riding on over to join the wagon's mounted escort on into town.

When Marley learned about Douglas McTavish he had decided this was probably the only chance they'd get to be local heroes so after he had listened to Steenan and Jones, he had told his riders what they would do.

Nathan was disgusted, now that most of his anger had worn itself out. "You fellers went along with him like a gang of sheep," he exclaimed. "Since I left off range-riding and been freighting I've had a lot of chance to study rangeriders. You fellers confirm what I think of them, now: brainless, silly, stupid bunch of chicken-livered little kids that have went and grown into men!"

No one contested that hard judgement, but one rider, the man who had not made trouble for McTavish when the Indian had leaned on his horse, said, "How do you know what was goin' to happen if Jim Field really tried to drag that Injun?" The cowboy looked steadily at Nathan, who was older, thicker, and taller, but the cowboy did not act entirely fearful. "There might have been some resistance to that notion, mister. Not everyone who rides for Marley is a lousy bully."

Nathan did not respond. He stood gazing at the youthful cowboy though, and when Smoke called over that there was dust coming up the road from the south,

Nathan pointed a thick finger at the cowboy who had spoken up to him and said, "What's your name?"

"Tom Butterfield."

"You and your friends don't move away from the side of the wagon," stated Nathan.

Steenan groaned and pushed feebly on the ground to get his body shoved up into a sitting posture. His shirt-front was splattered and his mouth was swelling and turning purple.

He looked around from eyes that barely seemed to focus. Then studied the two nearby corpses as though he had no idea what had happened, and meanwhile Jasper Jones came on up from the south, leading all those runaways.

Jasper's reaction when he saw the dazed rangeboss was to rein down to a halt and sit up there staring, then to turn an accusing look upon Nathan and Smoke, who came forward to take the reins of the recaptured horses. "Who did that?" Jasper demanded. "What happened?"

Smoke said, "Ask *him*," and indifferently bobbed his head in Steenan's direction. "Get down off that horse and lend a hand loading those two dead ones in the wagon."

Jasper swung down but instead of obeying he went over and boosted Steenan to his feet, frowningly peered at the badly discolored mouth, and got a tight expression across his features. But he said nothing more and when Steenan was able to stand unaided Jasper came back and helped sling the two deadweights into the wagon. He also lent a hand at mounting the surviving rangeriders, and when Rand came over to also get astride Jasper helped him too. He did it all while wearing that bitter-eyed expression and neither Nat nor Smoke heeded this. They were not as opposed to Jasper as they were to the rangeboss, but they were not entirely favorable towards the cowboy either.

It was a unique cavalcade which finally resumed travel up the north roadway. Marley's surviving riders were disarmed and being herded along by Nathan Trumbull, who rode with a carbine across his lap. Rand Steenan and Jasper Jones rode out in front where Nathan had shrewdly ordered them to ride. There was enough bad blood now so that Nathan did not like the idea of the Tuttle ranch men being behind him, at the tailgate of the wagon where they had ridden earlier.

There was almost no conversation as they got rolling again, with a pair of saddled, riderless horses tethered by their reins to the tailgate-chain. Smoke did not object and evidently neither did his partner.

Eventually, Rand Steenan rolled and lit a smoke, and almost at once flung it away because the tobacco pained his mouth. Up overhead on the load again, Douglas McTavish kept looking out over the rearward countryside. The mystery was not how she had got up that close—the roadside grass this far from town was knee-high—the mystery was where she had left her horse. There were no trees closer than a couple of miles, and although there were several brush-stands, they too were quite distant. She could have crawled that far but it would have taken a lot of time and would have been a genuine hardship.

The secret was simple enough; out several hundred yards, and even in closer, there were vein-like erosion gullies ranging from three feet deep to eight and ten feet deep. Clearly the Sioux girl had left her horse down out of sight in one of those *arroyos*.

McTavish did not mention this. He in fact did not mention the girl at all and even when Smoke twisted on the seat to strike up a little conversation, McTavish only grunted. He was busy with his thoughts and had no inclination to talk.

They crawled through the golden day with the sun moving inexorably upon its overhead radius without seeing another human being. Even when Smoke surmised that they could be no more than perhaps five or six miles south of Meridian, they saw no one. Evidently the fright which had driven folks to cover was still holding them there. Maybe the people up around Meridian did not know the stronghearts had gone on southward, or maybe, knowing that, they still preferred to wait in their town where they had everything they needed and where there was no danger.

Smoke was whittling off a fresh cud when he remembered a cynical remark Rand Steenan had made about the people of Meridian. He cheeked his chaw, leaned out and looked back where Steenan was riding, one side of his face a mess; caked with dry blood, purple and badly swollen. Smoke had had in mind striking up a conversation but he changed his mind and straightened on the seat just as Jasper Jones threw up an arm to point.

Three horsemen were riding at a loose lope from the west across the stageroad towards the east, up where it was finally possible to see sunshine bouncing off corrugated tin roofs.

Undoubtedly those three riders had seen the freighter with its mounted escort. The fact that they would carry the news to town of the oncoming cavalcade without coming down for a closer look confirmed in Smoke's mind what Steenan had said about the Meridians being wary people.

He spat, not very concerned, and a little ruefully examined two torn sleeves in his shirt where both elbows had worn through the cloth as he'd crawled under the wagon back yonder. A single man's ordinary reaction to torn clothing was to shed it and buy new clothing. It was a waste of money, as Smoke knew, but the alternative—getting married so there would be someone to do the mending—was far more expensive. And it also had other disadvantages.

McTavish grunted so Smoke craned around, his grip on the lines slackening. As a matter of fact he could have looped them for all the difference his guidance from here on would have made; those mules out ahead had sighted the rooftops and would unerringly head for them, lines or no lines.

McTavish pointed. Far to the west, little more than a shifting shadow actually but discernible nonetheless, was a solitary rider, but it required concentration upon the exact area to make her out. Smoke nodded as he saw her and McTavish then jutted his jaw in the direction of the town.

"If I could ride I'd go out and at least ride with her," he told Smoke. "She is Indian."

Smoke considered that. The longer he dwelt upon it the more he felt responsibility; the girl had proven her valor and she had also proven her ability to shoot. Being as wary as she was and coming this close to a town which still considered itself at least in part under siege by Indians, could mean serious trouble for her. The moment she fled from townsmen or others who might be riding out and around, they would go in hot pursuit.

No doubt this was about what McTavish had meant when he'd mentioned riding out there with her. Smoke leaned to spray amber, hauled back upright and continued to narrowly look far out where the landforms changed from mile to mile.

"How can I get close enough to talk to her?" he asked, and McTavish shook his head.

"You can't," he replied. "I tried to explain that we were friends. She would not come any closer than the barn back yonder."

"Then how can we help her if some townsmen see her and make a run at her?"

McTavish sat propped against a burlap bundle looking out there and not saying a word. He was deep in thought, and no doubt he was also deep in worry, because those three riders they had seen shortly before sighting the girl were not the only scouts and horsemen fanning out to ascertain that the stronghearts were gone. Eventually, unless she gave up acting as a sort of ghostly escort for the freight outfit, she was going to encounter rangemen, possemen, or just curious townsmen riding out from Meridian. Right now was not a good time to look like an Indian. She rode astride so no one would think it possible she was not a male Indian warrior, and there were plenty of people who would not care what she was if they could line her up between a rear sight and a front sight.

Up ahead someone rang a bell. This distracted both McTavish and Smoke, at least for a moment or two, then McTavish returned to his former vigil but Smoke stood in the boot to look ahead.

Several townsmen were dead ahead on the outskirts of Meridian, armed, of course, but clearly very curious about the oncoming freighter and its riding escort.

As Smoke eased down he called to Nathan. When they were together alongside the rig Smoke said, "You better keep close watch on Marley's men when we go up the roadway. We'll need them to explain what happened and it'd be better if they didn't get to thinking they had a lot of friends in town or they'll start makin' trouble for you and me."

Nat had already arrived at this same conclusion, so when he rode ahead and herded the prisoners along with him, he warned them in his most growly tone of voice not to talk to anyone they saw in the roadway and not to draw rein until they were in front of the town marshal's office.

Those people up ahead who had been ringing the bell loomed up as local merchants. Smoke recognized some of them and nodded as he tooled the wagon right on up past the tar-paper shacks at the lower end of town, heading for the jailhouse which was midway along.

People came out of stores and residences and stared, mostly in silence, but occasionally someone would hoot or call to the men. When they reached the jail-house the large, portly, graying man out front with a badge pinned to his vest and with a shotgun hanging loosely in the bend of one arm, stepped from the plankwalk and strode into the roadway with an author-itative expression on his big round face.

Steenan and Jasper Jones halted ahead a few yards, but the lawman only nodded to them. He was heading for Nathan, still herding along the disarmed rangemen and still balancing a Winchester across his lap. Nat looked dour enough to be the head man, and as far as Smoke was concerned he could go right ahead and be the head man, but Smoke hauled the mules down to a halt and set the binders as the lawman curtly nodded and said, "You fellers have In'ian trouble, did you?"

Nathan shook his head looking almost antagonisti-cally back. "We had whiteskin trouble, Marshal, but no redskin trouble." Nathan jutted his chin. "These here cowboys and their boss tried to take a wounded In'ian away from us. Their boss and one rider is in the back of the wagon—dead." Nathan paused, watching the lawman's eyes widen. "These here are the leftovers, these three darned idiots are what's left after the smoke cleared and you're welcome to them. Where do you figure we'd ought to put Johnson Marley and that other dead one?"

The lawman said, "Johnson Marley . . . ?" And very slowly turned his head to the disarmed riders. "Dead . . . ?"

That youthful rider named Butterfield pointed. "In the freight wagon, Marshal. Him and Jim Field. It's a long story." Butterfield dropped his arm and almost reluctantly added a little more. "That feller is right, Mister Marley and us fellers was going to take a sick Indian these freighters have in the wagon, and hang him. The freighters resisted. And there was someone else, I think. I'm not sure about this but seemed to me when the shootin' commenced there was someone back a hundred yards or so behind us in the grass." Butterfield looked around for support and verification but all he got was blank looks so he said no more on this subject and when the lawman said, "It wasn't no In'ian attack, then?" Butterfield shook his head. "Never seen any In'ians, Marshal, except for that hurt one inside the wagon."

The lawman unslung his shotgun and gripped it in both hands. "Fetch him out here," he demanded. Nathan and Smoke did not move. They stared steadily from the shotgun to the face of the town marshal until Smoke drawled his suggestion that the lawman put that scattergun back in the crook of his arm and Jasper Jones surprisingly enough spoke up in support of this. He said, "No more guns, Marshal. You don't need it anyway, the In'ian's already been shot a couple of times. Put the darned shotgun away."

From the plankwalk behind the lawman a rough-voiced big, older man called roughly, "Do like they say, Jeff. Put the gun aside."

Whoever that gruff older man was, his words seemed to carry considerable weight because the lawman raised the shotgun and sank it again in the crook of his arm and as Smoke smiled, he also said, "Marshal; we need the doctor for our In'ian, and we need whatever else you got to take over those dead fellers in the back of the wagon—but mostly, Marshal, my partner and I need a place to park the rig and put up the mules, then we need a place to get something decent to cook."

That same gruff older man pointed. "Take your rig down to the public corrals, gents. I'll have feed sent along. Take your redskin down there too. I'll send the pill-pusher as soon as I can find him." The older man looked across the road where the local cafe was, and pointed. "Fill up over yonder—on the town, gents. My name is Mack Overman."

Mack Overman turned and walked up through the silent crowd, evidently bent on keeping his word about that feed, and about finding the medical practitioner.

Smoke and Nathan exchanged a look. Whoever Mack Overman was, he was exactly the friend they needed. Nathan growled for the Marley riders to dismount. He also told Steenan and Jasper to get down. Then he leaned and said, "Now you got some scum to point your pop-gun at, Marshal."

Smoke grinned and clucked up the mules. He had to make a walk to the end of town in order to have sufficient room to turn and head back to the lower end of town where the shoeing-works, the liverybarn, and the public corrals were.

10
A LINGERING PROBLEM

Human nature was hung up on a lot of idiosyncrasies, but the most demonstrable one was its capacity to be influenced. Fortunately for the men with the freight wagon down by the Meridian public corrals, the men who had ridden for Johnson Marley, influenced by the young rider named Butterfield, who related things precisely as they had happened and in this fashion established the precedent, told the town marshal and most of the interested citizens of Meridian what had happened and *how* it had happened. They had left Johnson Marley looking like a dead villain, which he probably deserved, and they had left Smoke and Nat looking like rugged, stubborn upholders of the kind of frontier virtue most folks believed in.

It was this change which had a little to do with how Smoke and Nat were welcomed to town, but most importantly this was the fresh influence which inhibited even the town's adamant Indian-haters, and there are always some of those in every cowtown, so that by the time the medical practitioner arrived down at the wagon camp a number of local people including a clerk from the general stores for whom Smoke and Nat had freight on board, came down with offerings ranging from bottles of pop-skull to baskets of home-cooked biscuits and even a large apple pie.

The doctor was a youngish man, nervous by temperament and quick in his judgments and his physical movements. His name was Ambrose Healy and although because of his thinness and his boyish features he looked young enough to have only recently graduated from medical school, he in fact was in his forties and had been in practice almost eight years, all of it around Meridian.

There were undoubtedly better physicians around, but not at Meridian, and as he worked over McTavish he demonstrated a capacity to be both gentle and experienced. For the chest wound he said candidly that if McTavish had not died up until now, and had not caught pneumonia or some other respiratory ailment, and had been able to move a little, weak though he was from loss of blood, he would survive. As for the gouge alongside McTavish's head Doctor Healy shook his head. The cemeteries were full of men whose skulls had not been thick enough to withstand the shock and stress.

Otherwise, he said, as Smoke and Nathan hunkered in afternoon sunlight holding tin cups of coffee which were half whisky, McTavish was going to have a very noticeable scar even if he learned to comb his hair over most of it.

As for the concussion which Smoke and Nathan had feared, Doctor Healy was sanguine. He did not know whether the skull had been cracked or not, but he thought not—or; if there had been a concussion, it had not been very bad, otherwise quite obviously Douglas would have been much worse off than he was. When Smoke mentioned how long Douglas had been only semi-conscious, Doctor Healy reaffirmed what he had just said, but added one more little item.

"I did not say he did *not* have a concussion, gents. It's probable that he did have. No one gets that close a call alongside the head from a bullet or a club, or even a bad fall, without having some kind of mental trauma." He looked at McTavish. "What I *am* saying is that it clearly was not the kind of concussion which causes death." Doctor Healy beamed a large smile. "He wouldn't be here, would he?"

Nathan's mood was still not the best. "Very funny," he said sourly. "What else?"

"Loss of blood," replied the doctor, his big smile winking out in the face of Nat's craggy regard of him. "The weakness, and no doubt many of the other symptoms you've described were the result of the general debility arising from losing too much blood. Yet, all in all, gents, your In'ian is in fair shape. He'll be weak and in need of lots of food and plenty of rest for several weeks, but he'll make it." Doctor Healy made a nervous little giggle. "He's a lot better off than those other two fellers, the ones they've taken off your wagon and delivered to my embalming shed."

"How do you know that?" growled Nat, and turned as Smoke rammed him with an elbow.

Smoke said, "How much do we owe you, Doctor?"

Ambrose Healy seemed more concerned in getting away from the vicinity of that scarred old wagon and those unshaven disreputable-looking freighters, one of whom was decidedly unpleasant. "Nothing," he said, nervously smiling again. "Nothing, this time, gents."

That gruff older man named Overman walked up as the doctor was departing. He eyed Douglas craggily, as though he might not be entirely fond of Indians, but when he spoke to Nathan and Smoke there was nothing mentioned to support this view.

"You got the mule feed, I see, and that was Healy just walkin' off," he said, coming in closer to the little guttering cooking fire to squat down. "I been up with the town marshal and those fellers from the Tuttle brothers' outfit." Overman looked with hard approval at the unshaven and unwashed freighters. "You did about right. Anyway, whatever the law decides, you got justification and those cowboys said so. As for the marshal—hell—he's not going to do anything."

"You're sure," stated Nathan. "He didn't act too friendly."

Overman pulled a long face. "He's all right. In fact he's a pretty sensible feller when he's steered right."

Nathan said, "And how about our redskin?"

Overman turned. Douglas was leaning against some

mounded horse-gear wrapped in blankets. He was freshly washed and freshly bandaged, thanks to Ambrose Healy, and he had been studying Mack Overman ever since the gruff old man had arrived in camp.

"It sure don't seem to me a feller could survive all that hauling around if he'd been shot up like your In'ian was. It just don't seem reasonable."

Smoke could easily concede this because he'd thought the same ever since he'd first looked down atop the wagon's load and seen that blood-splattered man lying there. "But he *did* survive it," Smoke said, jerking a thumb. "There he sits, with both eyes open and with his chest risin' and fallin'."

Overman scratched his ribs and frowned a little as he said, "Yeah, that is my point, gents. Here he is—and you know as well as I know that blessed few men have ever survived gettin' shot up like that." Overman raised grave eyes. "It just seems to me those folks might be right who said the redskin was *with* those Crows, not against them."

Nathan groaned aloud. "Not that crap again," he exclaimed. "Rand Steenan is an old granny. I thought so yesterday when we was holed-up with him and I still think so. Him and his cowboy. Mister, that redskin isn't even a Crow."

Overman nodded his head for the first time. He was older and he had lived through a lot of Indian difficulties. He had learned considerably about Indians like most folks of his generation had, not because they wanted to learn about them or because they felt any need to know about them, but simply because with Indians constantly close by, it was just unavoidable that stockmen and townsmen got to know quite a bit of their lore.

Overman proved that he was one of that earlier generation, when he said, "Yeah; he's a Northern Cheyenne. They was fightin' devils—worse'n their cousins the Sioux. He wouldn't want to be mistaken for a Crow any more'n he want to be mistaken for a digger In'ian, a mangy Shoshoni."

This, then, more than what he had heard or had been told, was evidently what had influenced Mack Overman in Douglas's favor, but he still looked skeptical. In fact, when he said, "All right; it happened like you fellers told it—but I'm going to be doubtful all the same."

Smoke had a question. "How doubtful, Mister Overman; doubtful enough so that when me and my pardner ride out this evening if folks come around to lynch McTavish you'd stand aside and let them do it?"

Both Nathan and Overman stared at Smoke. Nathan did not speak although he certainly looked quizzical. "No one's going to lynch anyone around Meridian," growled Overman. "There hasn't been a lynchin' around here in ten years. Folks don't much do that sort of thing any more. Your In'ian'd be safe enough. Now tell me: why are you boys going to ride out this evening?"

"There's another In'ian," Smoke said, and paused to

watch Overman's eyes widen a little. "We're going out and see if we can't make a council—do a little persuadin' talk."

Overman said, "What other In'ian? Those fellers at the jailhouse never mentioned another one. All they knew about was . . ."

Nathan said, "We're not askin' your help, mister, what Smoke wants to know is—will McTavish be safe?"

Overman stared at Nathan. "If you go ridin' out of here this late in the day, your In'ian'll be a hell of a lot safer than you'll be."

Nathan almost smiled. "That's a bloody fact," he said, and turned to refill his cup from the dirty little dented coffee-pot, and when this was done he looked across at his partner. "Thanks for talkin' it over with me first," he said.

Smoke was immune to Nathan's sarcasm because over the years he had developed an immunity to his partner's infrequent bad moods. He did not even reply, he simply leaned to pitch coffee-dregs into the fire making it hiss, then he slowly turned to glance all around. Until very recently there had been an occasional townsman or two saunter down to stand and stare. Now, evidently, local curiosity had been satisfied because aside from Overman there were no other Meridians around.

Over at the liverybarn someone was playing a harmonica—badly. Up the road in the direction of the harness shop, but opposite it no doubt where a saloon stood, a man called out in a clear, bell-like tenor, and got a gruff answer from another man, their greeting hinting that each was mildly surprised to see the other.

Then a woman laughed over opposite the liverybarn and up a few yards from the network of public corrals where some backyard fences screened garden patches and clothes lines and children's play areas. Her laughter held Nathan and Smoke silent and motionless for a moment. It was like listening to the liquid soft sound of a tiny waterfall on a very hot day.

Nathan shook it off and got stiffly upright, holding his tin cup. "Mister Overman," he said, "I got no idea what you do for a living but I can tell you for a blessed fact—it's better'n hauling freight no matter what it is."

"I own most of the buildings on the west side of town, Mister Trumbull," replied the gruff older man, also rising. "And I got a few on the east side. Just to set the record straight, I got my start freighting. Only in those days there was a hell of a lot more risk to it, and also a hell of a lot more profit; darned few men wanted to haul across hostile country even with an army escort. What you boys just been through was what old-time freighters went through every month in summertime, and now and again also during wintertime." Overman crookedly smiled at Nathan. "But chancy as it was in those days, gents, we never rode out after sundown when there was hostiles around. And those that did that—mostly they never came back."

Overman turned and looked down where McTavish was. "Don't fret about your tomahawk. I'll personally guarantee his safety. I'll have him hauled up to the stage-depot. That's where m'office is. I got the stage franchise." Overman grinned at Smoke. "I been thinkin' of maybe expandin' into the freight business a little."

Smoke sighed and pushed up off the ground too. "Sell you a fine span of mules and a pretty tough old wagon one of these days," he said.

A man wearing heavy cowhide boots came tramping in from the direction of the roadway. He was large and heavy and had a black spade beard. He looked more like a pirate than a merchant, but in fact his name was Mitchell Slidell and it was on several of the manifests Smoke and Nat had in their possible-box. He nodded all around, grunted something to Overman, and dropped a cigar-stub as he said, "You fellers got freight for me?"

They had. If they hadn't had freight for the general store up here they might not have come by way of the Meridian coachroad and if that had not obtained they would perhaps never have run afoul of those migrating, troublesome Crows.

"We'll haul it to your dock tomorrow," Nathan said.

Slidell was anxious. "It's all there? Didn't none of it get lost or plundered or anything?"

Nat raised his eyebrows. "No way for any of them things to have happened, mister."

"I heard you fellers was set upon and had to fight your way clear. The way they was tellin' it at the saloon . . ."

Overman interrupted. "The way they tell *anything* at the saloon, Mitch, is a lie and you'd ought to know it by now." Overman nodded and strode away. Slidell watched his departure briefly, then turned and said, "There's a lot of that freight I sure need at the store."

Smoke reiterated Nathan's earlier statement that they would hitch up and drive around to the opposite side of town tomorrow and unload at the dock out behind the store.

Slidell was satisfied. He seemed to loosen a little. "You didn't have no In'ian fight, then?" he said. "You didn't shoot one up and fetch him along with you for Doc Healy to patch up?"

Smoke looked over at McTavish. The Indian rangeman's dark features were partially obscured by the settling gloom of pre-dusk, but a faint, tough smile was discernible when he returned Smoke's look.

Nathan explained one more time that McTavish had been shot by the break-outs, then he also said, "Go hunt up Marley's riders for the story of the fight. It wasn't with In'ians it was with whites."

Slidell might have lingered but Nathan turned towards the mule corral and Smoke sauntered over in that direction also. They stood, backs to the camp, until the storekeeper had also departed, then they returned, looked down, and Smoke said, "Douglas, you heard Overman. You'll be safe. If you aren't, when we get back we'll level their gawddamned town."

McTavish was either unworried or chose to hide it, but in either event he ignored the question of his personal well-being to say, "You'll never find her. Especially you won't find her in the dark. And if you get too close . . . why don't you wait until tomorrow and maybe we could get a wagon and I could go out there with you? If she saw me . . ."

"If we wait until tomorrow," stated Smoke, "someone else is going to find her first. I don't care how good she is at hiding and fading away; up here around Meridian there will be folks riding back and forth more than ever, now that the broncos are gone, and someone sure as hell will stumble over her. And if they don't shoot her she might shoot them. That's what we'd like to prevent." Smoke regarded the Indian for a moment. "You can help. Tell us the best way to find her."

"Take a spare horse," said McTavish. "See if they got a horsin' mare at the liverybarn and if so, take it along and when you figure you might be far enough out, turn the mare loose, then listen for it to sniff up her mount and whinny. Then follow it on in—and she'll shoot you."

Smoke smiled. "Thanks, Douglas. You're a real help." He and Nat turned to head over in the direction of the liverybarn. They had no intention of riding their own saddle animals. Enough was enough for the livestock they'd been using the last few days.

11
INTO THE NIGHT

Nathan and Smoke got along so well because as a general rule what one suggested the other one was amenable to. As Nathan indicated now, when he said, "It might work better at night anyway. One darned sure thing, if she's distracted by a horsing mare we might get her first. In daylight it wouldn't even work."

The horsing mare was an old spotted horse, sorrel and white. She was just ugly enough to confirm the convictions that among animals personal attractiveness had nothing at all to do with the mating urge. She clearly had had her share of colts.

The liveryman who handed up the lead-rope had told them that if they did not bring her back they would only owe him ten dollars, and Smoke had retaliated by saying anyone thinking that ugly old spotted mare was worth more than two dollars deserved to get her back.

She was one of those mares that horsed hard. There was nothing demure about her at all, and as they led her away behind two rented geldings she did her best to arouse the interest of the geldings, and when this earned her simply a couple of disgusted looks, she hung back on the shank and whinnied, then she lunged ahead and whinnied again. Nathan had his dallies so she was unable to get free, but as he kept them tight he said, "That darned Douglas and his ideas!"

Smoke rode, said very little, chewed and when his partner finally got a sufficient interlude to permit him to roll a smoke, Smoke said, "The idea is to come onto this female warrior without her knowing we're around. You light that smoke and she'll either catch the match-glare or she'll smell the smoke."

Nathan said something under his breath and flung away the half-rolled cigarette.

The land west of Meridian was mostly flat with a little roll to it, and with some erosion ditches which the horses either were familiar with from previous excursions out here, or which they could sense well enough in advance to avoid them.

Only once did their animals take an interest in one of those ditches. That was when the horsing mare started nickering again and swishing her tail and acting giddy. Nathan guessed the reason for this. "The girl was out here. She was down in this arroyo, most likely watching us when we arrived in town."

They had to ride half a mile up-country to find a decent trail down into the arroyo and up the far side. Then they turned southward again, but on an angling course which was about equal parts westerly.

For a while the mare was tractable. They assumed—correctly—that she was fresh out of scents. For a while they rode on their angling course, then turned almost due west and tried that for another half or three-quarters of a mile. Again the old spotted mare hiked along as though she was not in heat.

Nathan halted, sat his horse for a while simply

looking and listening, then clucked up the livery animals and turned more to the northwest.

Smoke was amenable. He did not even ask why Nat had wanted to change course. He chewed, spat, rode loosely—and when the spotted mare threw one of her prancing, squalling, tail-wagging fits, Smoke considered the direction of her interest, then nodded at his partner.

Nathan leaned to tug loose the lead-shank. For a few moments the spotted mare did not realize she was free. She still cavorted and turned back towards Nathan. Then she found out there was no rope under her jaw, and with a loud squeal she whirled and started almost due northward in a loud, uninhibited rush.

The mounted freighters utilized her racket to mask their own, and although they were actually unable to make much noise, they wanted the sound of the shod hooves under them to blend with the cacophony of hoof-sounds the mare was making.

She had clearly picked up the scent of another horse. It was improbable that it was a stallion despite the silly way the mare was acting. On the other hand it was entirely possible that what she had located was someone's range loose-stock; turned out using horses from some ranch, or perhaps cut-backs from the ranches those Crows had raided.

She whistled like a wild mare, then she trumpeted. Not until she had raced along almost a full mile and had left no doubt in the ears of any listening creatures for a mile in all directions that there was a horsing mare in the area, did she slacken off a little, both in her whinnying and in her headlong rush.

Smoke spat, halted to sit a moment listening, then leaned and said, "Close, Nat." in a very quiet tone of voice.

They looked for a place to leave their geldings, found a thornpin thicket, which would normally be the last place a man would tether his horse, climbed down and carefully left their rented animals tied over there. The only advantage to a thornpin bush for tethering live-stock was that if the animals had any idea what kind of sedge they were tied to—one with a thousand dagger-sharp long thorns of hardwood—they did almost no moving around. When the rider returned his horse was usually in precisely the same position he had been in when the rider left him.

Nat and Smoke assumed local horses such as the liv-erybarn critters they were straddling would know all about local undergrowth. Whether they did or not was the least consideration, however, as Nat and Smoke took down their carbines and struck out on foot in the wake of the mare.

She was no longer in sight, and she was no longer making noise, so they could only strike out in the direction where they had seen her last.

They walked with a dozen or so yards separating them, and they were quiet. So was the night, so was the area on all sides of them right up until they encoun-tered a low, rolling dished place where the range swept away on the far side of a low landswell in all directions, several feet lower than the surrounding area, and here they could hear a flowing watercourse, a small but lively creek somewhere ahead and to their right.

Instinctively they swerved in search of the creek. People camped close to water every chance they got, and even if there was no camp along the creekbank somewhere it was reasonable to assume that spotted mare had gone over there to drink.

They were roughly a mile from the thicket where they had left the horses when up ahead a horse squealed in annoyance. It was exactly the tell-tale kind of sound they had been hoping for. It meant the spotted mare had located another horse.

They came closer in the darkness, strode ahead a short distance then stopped to listen. They did not hear anything. The mare was silent now and so was the horse she had annoyed, but there was the faint though unmistakable scent of a dying cooking-fire.

Nathan pointed and nodded his head as though he were satisfied the girl was up ahead along the creek in among the undergrowth and willows somewhere.

Smoke allowed his partner to lead on over there. When they were still closer and had an even better opportunity to pick up the cooking-fire smell, Nat waited and when Smoke came in beside him Nat jutted his jaw.

"Through the thicket yonder, a little northward. I saw a horse—looked bay or black—and the spotted mare is up there with him."

Smoke spat, dragged a soiled sleeve over his chin,

studied the dingy darkness up ahead where the irregular undergrowth girded the noisy little busy creek, and said, "She's a good shot and she's as spooky as a wild horse. What do you think?"

"Sneak in from north and south, then jump on her before she has a chance."

Smoke dryly said, "*If* she's asleep."

Nat thought she would be. It was late in the night and moreover she had selected her camp very well. A fleeing fugitive from the law could not have found a better hide-out. She would not be expecting an attack.

Smoke shrugged and turned to take the southerly approach. Without a word Nat struck out briskly to circle far out and around in order to be able to come down from the north.

Smoke had to kill a lot of time and even when he finally decided to start stalking the creek-willow camp, he had no way of knowing for a fact whether or not his partner was in place.

Of course he might be able to find the sleeping girl and jump her by himself.

He jettisoned the plug he'd been chewing since leaving Meridian, longed to rinse his mouth at the creek but instead started forward as soundlessly as he could, and nearly had heart failure when a big owl sprang into the air and frantically beat his wings to gather altitude and momentum. The man had not been one whit more startled than the big bird had been at finding a man slipping stealthily around out here in the night. The main difference was that the man fiercely swore under his breath and all the owl did was desperately struggle to get away from there.

Smoke had the acrid odor of the dying fire to guide him until he detected large animals moving and finally saw the spotted mare. She was with a powerful young horse, a gelding, judging from his silhouette and from the irritable way he was responding to the old mare's boldness.

The gelding seemed to be hobbled. Smoke was certain he was not tied because where they were standing, he and the old mare, there was nothing to tie a horse to.

Through the screen of underbush and willows there was a fine little grassy clearing perhaps two acres in size. The camp was out there, for a certainty, although Smoke did not make it out until he was able to very soundlessly and cautiously get right on up to the final round-about growth and halt to slowly block in particular areas of the star-lighted little clearing.

If there had been a moon it would have helped a lot. Since there was none, and since the stars were only an indifferent source of light, Smoke had to surmise through his own experience that the foremost lump out there in the tangled tall grass was the girl in her robes, and nearby would be the mounded horse equipment and perhaps whatever else she was carrying; parfleche bag, clothes-roll, perhaps her weapons.

He lifted his eyes to gaze out across where Nat would be coming down to get close. There was nothing to be seen or heard. He felt that Nat would not be along for another few minutes and with that much time to kill he started a very careful stalk on around to the east, following in and out among the protective undergrowth to get closer to the creek, which happened to also be where that slumbering lump was.

The horses either detected shadowy movement or picked up his scent. They watched him with frank interest but did not fidget particularly nor whinny at his presence, things for which he was grateful.

The noisy watercourse helped, but even so Smoke moved with vast patience. He did not move one foot until he'd placed the foremost one down and had tested it with all his weight to be sure there would be no snapping of dry twigs or rustling of old leaves. It was a painstaking slow way to get close but it was the only way unless of course he had chosen to aim his carbine and break into the clearing full of fight, in which case he might very well have roused someone who would have come up shooting.

A nightbird whistled its mournful call.

Smoke paused, studied the northward area where that bird was roosting, and offered no return-call. It had been a sound he and his partner had perfected between them over the years, so now Smoke increased his stalk a little. When he was as close as it was possible to get without leaving the protection of the undergrowth, he stopped, grounded the carbine, leaned down on it and made a closer study of the lumps out there.

The nightbird sounded from a different direction, which diverted Smoke long enough for the old mare to coyly bite the annoyed gelding and his reaction to this bold invitation was to whirl on his hobbled front legs and aim a kick which landed with very little actual force against the mare's ribs, but the sound was like someone striking a bass drum.

The mare was rebuked but it did not seem to deter her at all, she started over to bite the gelding again and this time he hopped out of reach.

Smoke felt like flinging a stone at the mare. Instead he tried to pick up his train of earlier thought about the fresh location of the nightbird.

Someone over among the pair of unkempt lumps upon the ground made a half-roused sound, then pitched over into a fresh position and went back to sleep.

Smoke held his breath until he saw Nat, finally, over in the misty shadows upon the very edge of the little clearing. He chanced exposing himself too, in order that Nathan would know where he was.

Nathan raised an arm, very slowly, to signal understanding, then lowered the arm and began his own trip on around the small clearing to join his partner.

It took almost a full fifteen minutes for the partners to be close enough to nod and point, then Smoke held up a hand for Nat to remain where he was, with his Winchester, while Smoke went ahead into the clearing to seek and appropriate the arms of the person out there blissfully sleeping in the tall grass.

It was close to midnight. Perhaps a little past midnight, in fact, and although the night was still pleasantly warm, it seemed upon the verge of changing, of becoming colder. Smoke got close enough to see blankets pulled over a dark head. At least someone was comfortably warm and intended to remain that way.

12
A NIGHT WORTH REMEMBERING

Smoke got up close enough to the foremost bundle to see a steel butt-plate. He leaned and very gently closed strong fingers around the stock. The gun was outside the blankets, partially covered. If there was also a six-gun he did not see it. He thought it probable the six-gun would be inside the blankets and robes where most campers kept their handguns—available for instant use.

He had the carbine worked free and was straightening back when someone moaned, and the hair along the back of Smoke's neck stood straight up. The sound had come from behind him and to one side, over where that second bundle was.

Smoke turned from the waist, still clutching the carbine. That was not a mound of saddlery and camp equipment, it was another slumberer wrapped in robes and blankets.

There were two of them!

Smoke was between them with his heart in his mouth when the old spotted mare slipped in unobserved and bit the hobbled gelding on the rump, hard. The gelding reacted with a violent kick and a sudden lunge as he tried to come swiftly around to retaliate further. The kick missed because the mare had anticipated it and was moving away immediately after biting the horse, but when the gelding lunged he demonstrated that he was an experienced horse. He sprang at the mare and spitefully lashed out, both ears pinned back, and bit her on the neck. It was not the same kind of attention-getting bite she had given him. The gelding bit down with full force, then he shook the mare as though she did not weigh about nine hundred pounds.

She squealed, threshed left and right, and when she finally freed herself she squealed again and swung to deliver a kicking broadside.

No one could sleep through all that bedlam. The person behind Smoke came up out of the robes and blankets like a turtle, head first, up and moving left and right to discover the cause of the commotion. Fortunately, the camper was looking in the opposite direction. But his friend wasn't; when that sleeper raised up the first thing to come into view was Smoke Lunceford standing there, half crouched, holding a Winchester in his hand.

It was a man, not a girl, and he reacted with a bawling big curse and a lunge inside his bedroll for the sixgun down in there.

Smoke had one second to do something. He swung the carbine, caught the man at his feet alongside the head, and the man toppled sideways. Smoke swung his entire body towards the other one, who was also a man, but this one was too astonished to react. He sat there, blankets down around his waist, mouth agape, staring. Smoke said, "Put both hands on top of the blankets!" The stranger obeyed, still looking too dumbfounded not to obey. "Keep 'em there," commanded Smoke, flung aside the Winchester he had so deftly picked up, then turned and fled back over into the trees and underbrush where Nathan was waiting. Nathan had been equally as astonished to find that instead of one Indian girl, what they had encountered was not a girl at all but two men.

They hastened as quietly as possible on around the south side of the clearing and when they were in the clear they ran a hundred yards, then dropped down to a jog and kept that up until they were almost back to the thornpin thicket where the horses were standing.

"Didn't you see two bedrolls?" demanded Nathan, sounding disgusted.

"I made out one bedroll and a mound of camp equipment," stated Smoke. "What the hell! You were standing right there too."

That was the end of it. Nathan could have argued. All that would have ensured was that his partner would argue back. They got astride the livery horses and angled westerly until they figured they were better than a mile out, well clear of carbine range, then they circled back towards the creek again, and this time Nathan lit up, exhaled bluish smoke in the cooling darkness—and softly laughed.

Smoke was not ready to go quite that far yet. He got a chew pouched into his cheek, spat, considered his amused and relieved partner, then said, "Now we're out the stupid mare."

"That feller you hit—when he comes round and the other one tells him there was a big evil-lookin' individual standin' over him . . ." Nat bowed low laughing again.

Smoke was still not ready to laugh. "Evil-lookin' . . . ?" He shrugged that off. "What about the ten-dollar old mare?"

As though this were her cue, the mare could be heard now racing northward over alongside the creek. Evidently those two bewildered campers had choused her out of their camp.

Nathan said, "Let's go. She's got to lead us somewhere."

Smoke did not retort although he most certainly could have. They loped eastward until they were within hearing-distance of the creek, then swung northward, and the mare suddenly detected them behind her and slammed down to a sliding halt. In her quest for a stallion she was even inclined to overlook the scent of two-legged creatures on the backs of the horses she heard. But when she waited, then caught a sighting, she turned up-country again.

Nathan said, "I never shot a horse in my life, but you're lookin' at one I'd cheerfully shoot right this minute."

They were parallel with Meridian, but well northward, as well as westward, of the town. It was a vast territory on all sides of them. Vast and dark-coated and hushed. They still had a hope that the mare would locate another horse and home-in on it for them, but after an hour of steadily shagging in her wake Smoke hauled down to a rambling walk, spat, shook his head in Nat's direction, and said, "This will go on all night—us and that silly old mare—and come dawn we'll simply be six or eight miles on towards the mountains without no In'ian girl."

Nathan agreed, and the following moment the mare nickered, then picked up the gait and went rushing headlong towards some distant scent.

Smoke said, "I hope it's a hundred foot hole in the ground."

It wasn't, it was another horse, and when Nathan turned cautiously in that direction half expecting it to be either another hidden camp of rangemen, or perhaps a remuda of someone's loose-stock, a solitary animal called shrilly to the spotted mare.

Smoke said, "Another mare." He had made that judgment from the tone and timbre of the distant animal's sound and he was correct but it would be a little while before he knew it, and meanwhile Nat tried to estimate the distance to the position of the second mare. When Smoke said, "She ain't moving," Nathan was encouraged to believe it was indeed a tethered or hobbled animal. He turned to look for a place to tie up, and there was nothing—no trees nor thickets, not even a thornpin hedge.

They dismounted and stood at the head of their horses, waiting. It did not take long. The mares found each other and squealed. It was easy to imagine them baring their teeth, putting back their ears, cake-walking and whirling as though to strike or kick.

Smoke shook his head and started walking forward to lead the way. Like many lifelong stockmen, he had no use for mares, even good-using ones.

They walked up a slight incline, which actually was the northernmost lip of that immense bowl they had earlier descended into. The mares were making spiteful little squeals at each other now. The noise was not especially loud, nor did it have to be for the two cautious freighters to use it as their guide.

This time, when they were barely close enough to make out the spotted mare, they could also see the other animal, but no sign of a bedroll on the ground out through the tall grass, and yet the mare which had attracted their spotted horse scantily moved. She was hobbled, but evidently she was not familiar with this variety of restriction because she barely moved her front legs at all.

Somewhere, there was a camp. Any animal as afraid of hobbles as this one was had not hopped very far from the site where a rider had buttoned the hobbles into place.

Smoke started to hand his reins to Nat, but the shorter and thicker man reversed the process with a curt remark. "You done it last time."

Nathan left his Winchester in the saddle-boot. They both could have done that back yonder where they had stalked those two rangemen; the range would not be any greater than a sixgun could take care of this time, either.

Nat was very quiet for a man of his beer-barrel build and heft. He had reason to be; sooner or later they were going to find a light sleeper, and the situation could very easily become deadly when that happened.

Nat got far enough ahead so that he could not see Smoke and the saddle animals behind him, nor the sleeper up ahead, all he could see was those two mares, and it turned out that the other mare was also horsing. Maybe she hadn't been, but the arrival of the strong-smelling spotted mare had brought her in. She was beginning to act roguish too, and perhaps that was a blessing because neither she nor the spotted mare paid the least attention to the thick, crouching man-shape which was east of them but well within their view.

Nat made a big half-circle—and found the camp!

It was over along the rising undulation where the immense bowl-shaped depression ended and the upper level land began again. He saw it because there was nothing to interfere with the sighting. The person who had selected that site had unquestionably done so because they commanded a completely unobstructed view in all directions—by daylight.

What Nat was attempting now he could not have come close to doing before sundown. There was a fine chance that he could not do it now, either, if those silly old mares had roused the camper over yonder.

He sank slowly to one knee in the high grass and waited for some sign of life out where the dark spot was upon the gentle low slope.

There was nothing to be seen, no movement of any kind. He went a little closer and sank down soundlessly again. He angled so as to get between the hobbled mare and the distant camp, and, of course, that cut off whoever was over yonder on the slope from the hobbled horse.

He eased out his sixgun, held it low and gently cocked it, then he arose and progressed another few yards before sinking down in the grass again. He did that six times before he was close enough to the sidehill-camp to make out one pile of robes and one saddle beside it. But the starlight was not good enough to let him see much more, so he arose the last time and stalked ahead, got within fifty yards, and leaned to peer dead ahead.

Behind him and to his right something rustled suddenly in the grass. Nat did not turn, did not make any attempt to even swing his head, he hurled himself sidewards and landed rolling.

Someone's carbine barrel hit the ground with enough force to make a reverberation that Nat felt, and he increased the speed of his rolling retreat.

Someone came ahead in a savage rush and swung again. This time he saw her, did not recognize her except by a big-breasted silhouette as she had the Winchester above her head, and he suddenly changed course and desperately hurled himself at her legs.

The Winchester was starting to descend when his solid weight caught her on both shins and buckled her forward in a frantic attempt to jump across him. The

Winchester hit the ground within inches of Nat's legs and the girl's supple, strong body bounced off him and flipped sidewards. She too was desperately struggling to get clear.

Nat was a lithe man for someone of his build and size, and while the girl who was nowhere nearly as thick nor heavy could have probably moved much faster, Nat had the advantage of already being in the process of twisting, with both arms outstretched, when the girl started to frantically roll. He caught her shirt and held on. She aimed a savage kick and missed, so she aimed another one and that time although she connected Nat had his powerful thigh turned and the blow glanced off. Then he growled as she abruptly abandoned her tactic of flight and escape, and lashed out at him with both hands formed into claw seeking his eyes.

He dropped his head forward, felt the stinging rake of fingernails across his scalp through his hair, and ruthlessly wrenched the girl half around, then flung her sidewards and dartingly released his grip on the shirt-front and dived across her to pin both arms to her sides.

She arched beneath him, tried to use both knees in his groin, then tried to use them in his stomach, and when he dropped his full weight athwart her pinning her to the ground and making it impossible for her to use her legs, she suddenly stiffened both shoulders, raised her head and Nat heard powerful teeth clash when she missed his ear.

He pushed his body around until she was fully

beneath him with both arms pinned to the ground at her side. He raised his head for the first time to risk a look, and she tried to bite his cheek, then his nose.

He dropped his head and butted her under the chin. It must have dazed her; he felt all the fierce fighting stiffness momentarily go out of the body under him. He raised up again to look, and she glared upwards with a dull stare.

He said, "For Chris'sake stop fighting. I'm not going to harm you. I'm one of the freighters who own that wagon you put McTavish in."

She was breathing hard, and as the dazed interlude passed some of the tenseness returned to her body. He eased off, to one side, but did not relinquish his grip on both of her wrists. Then he gave the nightbird call, twice, one call following immediately after the other one.

She twisted to look southward, then she tried to free her wrists. Nat held her motionless without much effort. He had the power of a bear.

"Do you understand?" he asked her. "Did you know what I just told you? We are not your enemies. We came out here to find you before some possemen or rangemen found you. Do you understand me?"

She stopped struggling but all the tenseness did not leave and moments later when Smoke appeared with their two horses, the tenseness returned fully and Nathan shook his head at her. Then he looked up. "I don't think she knows what I'm tryin' to tell her," he said.

Smoke scoffed. "She knows. Douglas said she was raised in a mission school like he was."

Nathan had forgot. Now he sat back pulling the girl up into a sitting position by the wrists. When Smoke said to let her go Nathan growled his retort.

"Like hell. She kicks and bites and scratches and uses her fists."

Smoke knelt in the grass on the girl's other side. He said, "McTavish is waiting in town to hear that we got you before some manhunter did it first. Listen to me—you're going back to Meridian with us."

She stiffened before their eyes and turned a look of absolute horror on Smoke. "No!" she exploded at him. "No!"

Smoke sighed. "All right. You don't go back to town with us, but lady, they'll eventually catch you out here and the mood folks are in today, they'll shoot first and look afterwards . . . You just plain are not safe out here."

"I will go to the northward mountains, and wait," she said, speaking so fast all the words ran together.

Smoke frowned. "Wait for what?"

Nathan released her wrists as he looked disgustedly at his partner. "For Douglas—what else."

Smoke looked at the girl. She was very pretty, even in the darkness. He tried to be gallant by saying, "Yeah; if I was Douglas I'd go find her in the mountains in a minute. But I'm not Douglas, and he didn't say he'd hunt her up when he got able to ride again."

"I'll wait anyway," she said, looking Smoke squarely

126

in the eye. "I'll watch all the roads and trails. When he comes, I'll ride down to him."

Smoke looked past her. He wondered whether she could actually make it that far without being caught and killed by irate stockmen or townsmen. Nathan nodded his head slowly. He was sure she could make it.

Smoke said, "All right. But it won't be easy, lady, and maybe you're timid and scairt of towns and all, but with Nat and me you'd be plenty safe in Meridian. Then, when we pulled out you and Douglas could come with . . ."

"No!" she exclaimed. "I will ride all night and get into the mountains. You tell Douglas where I am and that I'm waiting. Will you?"

Smoke gravely inclined his head. "Yes'm, we'll tell him. But suppose he don't—well—all right, you be almighty careful though, you hear me?"

She looked at Smoke and shyly smiled, then she arose and walked away leaving them kneeling there in the buffalo grass.

13
A TIME TO MOVE

Nathan gingerly examined the top of his head where the Sioux girl had clawed him, and as they turned back in the direction of Meridian he said, "Gawddammit, I quit rangeridin' because I was tired of all the rough work and hardship and lack of decent meals and sleep, and because I figured a man's better off with a steady seven-to-six job."

Smoke who had not experienced the girl's ferocity and who was slightly more placid anyway, simply said, "Well; what are you squawkin' about?"

"Squawkin' about? You want to see where she liked to dang near scalped me with her fingernails, and how she liked to kicked me with her feet and her knees? And for what? This here is the second night without any sleep and this time we didn't accomplish any more'n we accomplished last night. Hell; compared to this kind of existence rangeriding keeps looking better and better."

"What you need," announced Smoke, "is a bottle of whisky."

"What I need," stated Nat, "is twenty hours' sleep, five decent big meals, and a side of a creek somewhere where the sun's been strikin' that water all day so's it'll be warm enough to take a bath in."

"What do you need a bath for, you're not going to get married."

The night was colder now. It was also layered in a kind of eternal hush. Not even foxes or coyotes were abroad, evidently, because all the way back to the outskirts of Meridian the pair of horsemen saw no sign of any kind of animal, large or small.

The nighthawk at the liverybarn was loudly snoring when those two unshaven, filthy, rumpled and unsmiling apparitions appeared out of the back alley, so they put up the livery horses themselves. About the old mare, they were not very concerned. If they had to, they'd pay for her in the morning. It had been worth her price not to have to lead her back.

They went out back and across to the area of the public corrals. The mules ignored them; they could have been sleeping, but the chances were just as great that they had been awakened by the arrival of their owners, and were now unwilling to acknowledge anything about it, which would be consistent with mule nature.

But Douglas McTavish was not asleep. He may have been, but he was not now, when Smoke and Nat eased down among the litter of their freighter-camp. McTavish raised up out of the jumble of robes and said, "You didn't find her."

Nat peered. "I thought Overman was going to have you hauled up to the stage company corralyard."

"I wanted to stay here. You did not find her did you?"

"Yeah, we found her, and I got scratches atop my head to prove it. Douglas, if you ever marry up with her take my advice—get yourself a pair of right sharp hoof nippers and pare off her blasted fingernails right down to the quick."

"If you found her, where is she?"

Smoke explained, because Nat was wrestling with his boots and otherwise preparing to climb into his blankets to sleep away whatever was left of the night, and when Smoke had finished McTavish said, "I'll find her in the mountains."

Nat conceded that, with a big yawn. "Sure you will

because she'll be watching for you, but the thing is until the bad feeling dies away after those darned Crows going through the country, if someone else finds her first. . . ."

Smoke scoffed at that possibility. "Naw, not her, Nat."

"We found her didn't we?" demanded Trumbull and his partner continued to be scornful when he replied.

"No, we didn't. *She* found *us*."

Nathan muttered something about nit-picking and turned away in search of his blankets. Smoke and Douglas continued to sit and talk for about a half-hour, then Smoke also rolled in. The last of them to lower himself into the warmth of robes was the Indian cowboy.

There was not much of the night left, and although the freighting partners got to sleep quite late, it was nonetheless more of a rest than they had got the previous night, so when dawn ultimately roused them with its town-noises, and they came up looking, and feeling, drugged and deeply tired still, they were able nonetheless to shrug it off as they pulled on boots and headed for the trough to wash.

Shaving could wait. They had in mind hunting up the tonsorial parlor to get shorn as well as shaved. That was one of the luxuries of arriving in a town.

Hunger struck right after they were cleaned up and made more or less presentable in fresh attire and with their faces scrubbed and their hair combed.

McTavish was lying awake in his soogans. He looked about the same, but upon closer inspection his dark eyes were more alert than before. They said they'd fetch him back some breakfast and went hiking together over across the road in search of the cafe.

Early though they were, they were not the first patrons of the cafe, whose steamed-up front window and whose interior aroma of frying meat and boiling coffee were the strongest assurances of another day having arrived. Elsewhere around town although there were some signs of life, the place was a long way from being fully geared up to welcome a new day.

Two townsmen were eating, gulping coffee at the big long counter, and discussing the topic which was still uppermost around town: those Crows which had passed through. One of them said he had heard over at the stage depot that two companies of cavalry were in hot pursuit, and that the stronghearts were running for Nevada. The other man digested this information with a growly grunt and said, "There's one right here in town, and after all the massacreein' and horse-stealin' and all them buzzards done, folks had ought to string him up."

The first man paused to slide a large piece of coarse dark bread around and sop up his steak gravy before replying. "Ain't a Crow from what I heard."

"Whatever he is they'd ought to string him up anyway," mumbled the other man. "One's as bad as the others."

Nat looked over as the cafeman brought their plates, acting as though he had not heard any of that, and around them half a dozen other diners acted the same way.

A large youngish man with a shoeing-apron round his flat middle arose to drop some coins and wink at the cafeman, then depart. Otherwise, though, the diners were hard at it. None would be ready to leave for some little time yet.

The cafeman went around refilling coffee cups and when he came down where Smoke and Nat were sitting he evinced clear knowledge of who they were. As he leaned to pour he also said in a soft tone, "In every roomful of folks there's at least one feller favors hanging just out of hand." He winked, finished filling the cups and would have turned away but Smoke said, "How about makin' us up a bucket of stew and some coffee and maybe a slab of pie. We got that terrible In'ian down at our wagon-camp."

The cafeman nodded and turned away through the clank of plates and eating utensils and the drone of breakfast talk up and down the counter. Where those two other men were sitting there was no reaction so evidently Smoke's words had not traveled that far.

The cafeman was at work behind his curtained off cooking area when that Indian-hater turned to his companion with another suggestion.

"Army ought to recruit a bunch of rangemen to run down them bloodyhands. Cowboys are a heap better at it than the lousy army ever was."

Something neither Smoke nor Nat knew, and probably some of the other diners also did not know, was that the cafeman had spent fifteen years as a horse-soldier, and while that lynch-talk had not set well with

132

him, this latest bit of spiteful derogation did not go down at all. He poked his head out the curtain and looked steadily at the unsuspecting, garrulous townsman, then he said, "Mister Bostwick, the army done a hell of a lot more than rangemen ever did—or than townsfolk ever did—and I got scars to prove I know what I'm talking about!"

That was all, and it was not hostile although the look on the cafeman's face was unpleasant while he had been speaking.

Someone chuckled and Smoke turned. Overman was down the counter sandwiched between two other hulking large men. He winked up at Smoke, stood up and dropped some silver beside his plate, stepped back from the counter and looked over where those two disgruntled men were sitting.

"You don't like redskins nor the soldiers—who's left, us town-fellers?"

A lot of heads came up and turned. The pair of men at the upper end of the counter ducked a little lower and became very busy with their meal.

Ten minutes later when it was safe to do so without attracting more attention, those two men paid up and slipped out. A few heads turned to watch them depart, but most of the diners had already dismissed both those men and their pithy comments long before.

The cafeman brought the stew pail, the coffee, and a big slice of fresh blueberry pie. When Nat paid him the cafeman shrugged wide bony shoulders.

"They don't really mean all they said. I know 'em

both. But those darned In'ians passin' through got everyone fired up to some degree."

Outside in the brightening new day with the promise of sunlight in the offing, Meridian was beginning to look pretty much as it usually looked.

By stepping down into the roadway on their way across, and turning a little to look northward, it was possible to see distant, sharp-etched golden-lighted huge mountains.

"Hope she made it," Nat said.

When they got down to the camp McTavish ate like a horse. It was the first time he had really demonstrated genuine hunger and while no doubt the fact that what he'd had offered to him before this morning was bad, hunger if it increased and ran on long enough, inspired a man to close his eyes to the quality of food sometime, and just eat to stay alive. But McTavish had had no particular appetite, probably because he had been feverish, and even though there had to have been some hunger, until right now he had not shown it.

Nat grinned widely, his first real smile in several days. He and Smoke exchanged a look, then went over to care for the mules and when they returned a little later, after having also gone to the liverybarn to pay for the horses they had rented last night, and for the old spotted mare, McTavish was standing up dressed and ready.

Smoke peered, then shook his head. "You can't walk that far—to them mountains yonder—not in your condition, and you don't own no horse to pack you."

Nathan concurred. "Sit down," he told the Indian rangerider. "Get more rest. What is the big rush for anyway?"

"The girl," stated McTavish. "I don't want anything to happen to her."

Both freighters could understand that, Smoke more than Nathan. Nat was still not reconciled after the way she had done her utmost to maim him for life, but he was prepared to be charitable this morning. He had slept, had been fed a decent hot meal, had drank fresh coffee and was now standing in fresh sunlight. No matter how evil a man's mood might be, the accumulation of all those coinciding factors was bound to improve it.

"Wait," he told McTavish. "Just be patient another few hours. As soon as we've off-loaded over in back of the general store and got rid of some other stuff around Meridian, we'll be pulling northward for the pass through the mountains. You understand?"

McTavish "understood" meaning that he agreed to be patient, probably because he had no alternative. He went out to lend a hand hitching the mules and harnessing them, but Smoke frowned and pointed to a place in the shade of the huge old wagon. "Sit!" Smoke commanded, and McTavish sat.

Nat's rough estimate was fairly accurate. They drove around to the far side of town, down the alley to the dock behind the general store, off-loaded, got their pay, and wheeled southward beyond town before they had sufficient room to wheel completely around, then they plodded back northward up the same alleyway, and made two more very brief halts, and were upon the northernmost end of Meridian the last time, with a full and expansive view of the immense lift and rise of open country dead ahead.

Nat bought a bottle of whisky and carefully wrapped it in burlap before placing it beneath the high seat. Otherwise, they had that food Rand Steenan's man Jasper Jones had left in the wagon, so along with their private caches of tobacco, they were sufficiently supplied with the basic essentials, which was all they ever had anyway.

They had not stopped to see the doctor. Smoke had thought about it and had tried to convince McTavish it would be a good thing. McTavish would not listen, and Nathan topped it off by saying, "There is almost nothing those money-grubbin' buzzards can do for a man that a man's carcass can't pretty well do for itself."

Smoke stood once and looked back. They were half a mile north of town by then, and no doubt there were people back yonder such as the town marshal, old man Overman, Jones and Steenan and those brushpoppers who had worked for Johnson Marley, who were also craning for a final look at the big old freight wagon.

Nathan, who was not an individual who spent any time thinking back, was already scanning the yonder mountains, and they were still fifteen miles from being into the foothills.

In fact at the rate their wagon moved they would be

doing very well if they reached the foothills before sundown. The chances were, light load or not, they would have to camp this side of the mountains and make the final haul up into the pass tomorrow.

That was perfectly agreeable to Smoke, up there on the wagon-seat with a bulge in his left cheek. It was all right with McTavish and Nat too, evidently, since neither of them fretted. Nor would it have done one bit of good if they *had* fretted. If there was one variety of animal—aside from Smoke Lunceford—which was absolutely indifferent to any need for haste, under any circumstances, it was a mule. And Smoke was tooling four of them along.

14
AN INTERLUDE IN BLUE

They made camp within cannonshot of the foothills, but even if they had got up through there, they still would not have been into the real mountains which stood another five or six miles away.

McTavish wondered aloud if the girl might not recognize the big old freight wagon and perhaps slip down the intervening distance in the night.

If she did it, she remained far out in the darkness because not only did she not personally appear but the mules and Nat's horse gave no indication that they had detected the presence of another animal.

Nat was of the opinion that, wary as she was, they would probably get well up into the pass before she showed herself. Then he and Smoke set about banking a little popping juniper or cedar cooking-fire while McTavish sat back in the reflected warmth wrapped in a blanket. He looked more Indian than ever, but he did not act like one. In fact he seldom showed Indian characteristics.

They were solicitous. They kept him as immobile as possible, insisted that he stay warm, and fed him when they thought there was a chance of getting food down him, and tonight, just before they fed him, Nathan dug out that whisky bottle with a broad grin, completely forgetting the outburst an earlier mention of hard liquor had caused.

McTavish would not touch the stuff. He started out in another harangue about the evils of liquor and until Nathan sighed and passed the bottle to Smoke, then they both turned their back on their Indian to lace their coffee, McTavish did not run out of breath.

They poured whisky into his coffee, too.

Later, while they were eating, McTavish got expansive. He talked about his childhood, about the parents he had never known and had only heard of from the mission priests and sisters. He also mentioned some of the cow-outfits he had ridden for and some of the adventures he'd had as a rangerider. Smoke looked at Nathan. They had put too much whisky into the coffee. Not too much for them, but clearly too much for someone who did not use whisky.

McTavish did not stop recalling his past and regaling his companions with mission-school philosophy until they were finished with supper and he moved back to the wagon-side again where reflected heat, plus a gutful of food—and whisky—turned him drowsy enough to grow silent.

After he had rolled into the robes beneath the wagon and Nat had made a smoke which he lit while gazing in the direction of the slumbering Indian, Nat said, "Too bad. He's a likable feller. Too bad he's going to spend the rest of his life cowboying. He likes it."

Smoke leaned to discreetly let fly with amber juice into the fire, then hauled back to say, "They take to it like ducks to water. You know why? I heard a feller explain it one time; because it's as close as they can come nowadays to their old way of jumpin' on a horse and going sashaying off over the countryside. It's a substitute for hunting, for takin' to the war-trail, to exploring and forever bein' on the move."

Nathan trickled smoke. "They can have it," he said, and Smoke cocked an eye at his partner.

"What's the difference between it and the way you and me live? Isn't any that I can see. Well; we don't ride in the wake of cattle and look at nothin' more inspirin' than the rear-ends of a lot of cattle, but I can tell you from experience the rear-end of mules don't make a man write beautiful poetry neither."

Smoke let a moment pass, then also said, "Steenan and his cowboy . . ." He shook his head. "And that crazy bastard named Marley. What kind of a man'll get himself killed because he figures he'd ought to ride into a town lookin' like a big In'ian-lynching hero?"

"That darned lawman back there wouldn't have been any better except for Overman," stated Nathan, and flicked ash as he twisted to look around before also saying, "I take it back; freighting is better'n living in a town and being around some of the kinds of folks we've run into lately. For company, I'll take the mules."

They rolled in, after banking the fire hopefully so that there might be coals left in the morning, and for the first time in many days slept early and did not awake until later than usual.

When Nathan raised up and looked around, dawn was near, the mules were grazing in close waiting for their ration of crushed barley, and his partner was already at work at their little fire.

Douglas had rolled his robes and was leaning where Smoke had ordered him to stay. He did not appear as though enforced inactivity were something he would ever very successfully adjust to.

Nathan sat up and reached for his boots. "No red-skins for a change," he said.

McTavish turned slowly.

Nathan made a feeble smile. "Didn't mean nothing," he assured Douglas, and tried over again. "No Crows around."

Smoke was in the act of pushing wood under the pair of well-matched speckled boulders he had their coffee-pot balanced upon when Douglas said, "Soldiers," and pointed northwesterly off the stageroad a mile or more.

Nathan came wide awake in an instant, and Smoke

swiveled where he was hunkering, to look, holding a stick of dry wood in his hand.

There were only two soldiers. Normally, under the kind of circumstances Smoke and Nat had just come through, when someone mentioned soldiers the normal reaction was to expect at least a company of them.

After a long interval of thoughtful study, Smoke faced forward again and poked the stick under the stones.

"Two, an officer an' his dog-robber. Now *that's* how to go after a big band of bronco break-outs."

Nathan had nothing to say for a long while. He sat there half-dressed watching the oncoming pair of horsemen, then he gestured without taking his eyes off the soldiers. "Douglas, climb up the tailgate and get inside the wagon."

McTavish sat a while also studying those riders, before he arose and moved off to comply. As he was disappearing inside the high-sided old wagon he called back to Nathan, "They'll see that blanket-roll where I slept last night."

Nathan stirred, finished making himself presentable then scooped up the bedroll and hurled it over the wagon-side. It must have come close because Douglas swore.

Smoke busied himself with breakfast and Nat shook his head as he put one set of utensils and the tin plate and cup which went with them back into the possible-box on the side of the wagon. "One lousy thing after another," he grumbled but actually there was no reason—at least not very *much* reason—to be worried. As far as they knew these were simply couriers or scouts, or perhaps an officer and his orderly in search of those soldiers it was rumored down in Meridian were pushing on in the van of the stronghearts.

Then the soldiers got close enough to hold their arms aloft in the traditional peace-sign, and Smoke got a good look at the officer. He was gray, grizzled, a captain in rank and wore one of those close-cropped beards of the kind made popular by President Grant.

The enlisted man with him, a sergeant, was about the same age and although he was clean-shaven, the hair over his ears under the cap showed an equal amount of gray.

When they rode up the officer loosened in the saddle, eyed the coffee-pot, looked slowly around the camp, then said, "Fine morning, gents. Going to be a fine day. You mind if we get down?"

No one minded. In fact Smoke offered them some coffee and breakfast. They accepted coffee although they had only recently struck their own small camp up-country a few miles.

The officer was Captain Horatio Bragg and his sergeant's name was Patrick Ryan. As they moved in closer to tether horseflesh to high rear wagon-wheels the captain asked if Smoke and Nathan had seen the break-outs. They hadn't. He then asked if they'd been inconvenienced by the fact that a large war-party of Crows had jumped the reservation, and this time Nathan gave a cryptic retort.

"We get inconvenienced, Captain, if it just rains very hard. Or if there's a grass fire in summertime. So I guess you could say we were inconvenienced a little by those redskins passing through. There's a town down yonder. Those folks didn't see any redskins either, but they were armed to the gullet and forted up."

Smoke changed the subject. "We heard there was an army detail chasing the Crows," he said, and let it hang there in case Captain Bragg chose to comment on it. He did.

"There is a cavalry *column* in pursuit," he said, emphasizing the difference between a detail and the larger "column". "They have some Indian scouts along. I'm sure they will overtake the break-outs long before they get down as far as Nevada. There is also another column coming north from Fort Carson. The strategy is to catch the Crows between the two columns." Captain Bragg looked straight at Smoke as he explained all this and in the very next breath, without a shred of warning he said, "Why are you hiding an Indian?"

There was no point in denying it and there was no point in asking how Captain Bragg knew they were hiding McTavish. Smoke felt inside a shirt-pocket for his plug and took his time about worrying off a corner, then offering the plug around. He got no takers and pocketed the plug, then he said, "Captain, we don't have to hide anyone. We've done no wrong and neither has the In'ian."

Sergeant Ryan dryly said, "And that'll be why you're

hiding him, buckos, because none of you has done any wrong?"

Nathan began to redden. Neither Captain Bragg nor Sergeant Ryan looked very friendly right now. "He's injured and he don't move around much. He's in the wagon, and if you're trying to make something out of that, Sergeant. . . ."

Captain Bragg turned dark, deep-set eyes upon Nathan. Captain Bragg did not look as though he were a compromising man. "Then you won't object if we talk to him," he murmured, and waited for Nathan's reply.

"Talk to him about what?" asked Smoke.

"About three murders of settlers in their beds up around the Staunton cattle country."

Smoke and Nat gazed at the officer without opening their mouths. Douglas had admitted to them that he had worked for some outfit up there called the Oak Cattle Company. It was improbable that Captain Bragg knew where Douglas was from, but if he *had* known he could not have caused any more of a misgiving among the pair of freighters than to mention what he had just told them.

Smoke said, "Captain, do you know a Cheyenne from a Crow?"

Bragg jerked his thumb. "Sergeant Ryan does. He's been fifteen years out here. Between Colorado and Montana. He even speaks some of their lingo. What about it?"

"Our redskin is a Cheyenne not a Crow. He is a mission-raised cowboy."

Sergeant Ryan spoke again in that dry voice. "From up around Staunton by any chance?"

Smoke answered that. "Yeah, from some cow-outfit up there called the Oak Cattle Company. And he didn't shoot any settlers."

"Is that so?" said the non-commissioned officer in that same infuriating tone of voice. "How do you know he didn't shoot anyone up there?"

"Because he was shot by the Crows alongside the head, they hauled him along as a hostage. He was also shot through the lungs. Fellers used up like that don't go riding around shooting folks, do they?"

"If he was wounded at the last ranch," stated Sergeant Ryan, "it's possible he was one of those raiders."

"They were Crows. I already told you he was a Cheyenne," exclaimed Nathan and before a genuine argument could begin, Douglas came around from the rear of the wagon. His head was bandaged and there was obviously another bandage under his shirt as he stepped over alongside a high near wagon-wheel and leaned there while he studied the captain and the sergeant.

Sergeant Ryan spoke in Dakota. "Are you armed?"

A Northern Cheyenne could understand and speak the language of the Sioux, but Douglas McTavish couldn't because he had never learned any language but English, so he stood gazing at the sergeant without replying.

"Do you have a gun in your clothing?" Sergeant Ryan asked in English.

Douglas shook his head. "No. And I didn't shoot

anyone. I was sitting on my horse. The Indians came out of the trees. I sat there watching them. I had never seen a real war-party before, not even when it was only Crows. I was watching and they shot me. That's all I know until these men cared for me where the Crows put me down, finally. That's the truth."

Captain Bragg was clearly intrigued by an Indian who could not speak an Indian language and whose English had none of the unique little accented inflexions other Indians spoke with. He relaxed a little and fished inside his tunic for a thin cigar which he lit from the coals of the fire. He seemed to be a rational, reasonable man, and perhaps most uniquely of all, he showed no army-bias. After more than a generation of suffering humiliations, defeats, and murders at the hands of the Indians, the army through its commissioned officers—and a great many of its enlisted men—was fiercely and uncompromisingly anti-Indian.

Bragg gestured. "Sit down," he said to Douglas, indicating a place by the little fire, but McTavish had had plenty of reason lately to be leery and for all any of the others knew, including Smoke and Nat, he could have had that deep-down, ingrained fear of blue uniforms most Indians had, but in any case he remained over where he was against the rear wagon wheel.

Bragg did not press it. He looked relaxed as he trickled fragrant cigar smoke and made a long study of McTavish before also saying, "I believe you. Would you like to know why? I'll tell you, but first I want you to tell me your first name. Just the first name."

Douglas looked narrowly at the officer, as though perhaps he did not understand him or perhaps as though he were becoming increasingly suspicious of him. "My first name is Douglas."

Captain Bragg cast a sidelong glance at Sergeant Ryan before saying, "And your last name is McTavish."

Even Smoke was surprised, and he was not an easy individual to startle. None of them had told Captain Bragg what Douglas's name was. The odds against someone arbitrarily selecting a name like that for a full-blood Cheyenne had to be astronomical.

Bragg smiled through bluish cigar smoke. "You are one of the people reportedly murdered by Indians up around Staunton," he said, and shook the empty tin cup in his fist until Smoke caught the implication and leaned to lift the pot and refill the cup.

Sergeant Ryan was impassive. After his officer was sipping coffee, though, he said, "You got proof that your name is Douglas McTavish?"

Nathan looked as though his patience had reached its end. He may have been sorting through thoughts to find words adequate to the way he felt, when McTavish answered the sergeant.

"My name is tattooed on my back."

Ryan sighed and held up a hand as Douglas started to straighten up off the wheel as though to shed his upper garments. "If you know that," the sergeant said, still in his dry voice, "you'll be McTavish."

Captain Bragg finished his coffee and stood up. He was not quite as tall as Smoke but he was taller than

Nathan, only less than half as thick. "Been nice talking to you gents," he said, amiably, and turned to wink over at McTavish. Then he jerked his head and the sergeant went over to fetch in their horses.

The last thing the captain said as he was settling across his McClellan rig and was evening up his reins, was spoken to McTavish in a kindly voice.

"Don't go back up there. I mean Staunton; stay away from the area around there for six months or so. There is an awful lot of bad feeling. The Crows hit those ranches pretty hard up there. Not everyone can tell a Crow from a Cheyenne."

Captain Bragg touched his hat-brim to Smoke and Nathan. "Right obliged for the coffee and the conversation, gents." He led off and his dog-robber loped in his wake a decent interval for an enlisted man. The dog-robber did not look back, which was probably just as well because neither the Indian back there nor the pair of freighters felt very kindly towards him.

Smoke turned back to the fire. "Let's get the hell on up into the pass," he said, and started kicking dirt over their little fire.

15
TOWARDS THE RIMROCKS

The mules walked sturdily along. It helped that the load had been lightened considerably back at Meridian because once they started up through the foothills the roadway tilted more and more, all the way to the forested mountain flanks, and from there on the pass would alternately dip and rise.

Nat was the outrider, as usual. Smoke sat upon the high seat looking around as they began wheeling past the last open, grassy and undulating lower foothills.

The mountains were never very warm until about ten or eleven o'clock in the morning. Their forests precluded sunrays from reaching the roadway for quite a while. In fact when Smoke set his hitch to the first climb there were shadows on all sides and the air down in there was still cold.

Nathan went ahead half a mile, sat his horse scanning their back-trail from that uphill point of vantage, then turned and walked part way back, until Smoke and the outfit hauled on up to him. He was lighting a smoke when he said, "Hey, Douglas—you better sit up there atop the load where she can spy you. Sure as hell if she just sees me and Smoke she isn't going to turn up."

It was good advice, although the commentary which went with it did not have to be correct; she knew their wagon by now; whether she saw McTavish or not she would know he was there.

A morning stagecoach rattling down the hill, binders set just tightly enough so that, although the rear wheels were not skidding, there was a little slack in the traces, meaning that the driver was not allowing his rig to ride up onto the heels of his horses.

He and his gunguard were bundled in mothy-looking old buffalo coats. Their hats were pulled low and the driver had a muffler stuffed into the throat of his upturned coat-collar. As he guided his vehicle out and around the much larger freight wagon he raised a gloved hand in high salute and called over a friendly big booming greeting to which Smoke responded the same way. There was no room to halt, otherwise, if the coach were not running to a schedule, both outfits might have stopped long enough to exchange news.

Nathan was at the side of the road in some trees. The driver and guard must not have seen him. They had seen McTavish though, after they passed down the side of the wagon, and after they had saluted Smoke, because they both turned to briefly stare before the demands of their six-horse hitch out front required their fresh attention where the road began to let up a little.

When they got down to Meridian they would hear the story. By now it was probably common knowledge all over the Meridian countryside, and also by now it had probably begun to accumulate the inevitable embellishments which accrued to such a tale.

Neither of the principals, Nat Trumbull nor Smoke Lunceford, were concerned. They did not even think back to their earlier adventures. They had just one more obligation—or responsibility—then they were out of it, and free to pick up their meandering lives where that first sighting of Indians had changed things.

For a while it seemed that they would never find the girl. Smoke did not comment but Nat did; he was afraid she might have been captured by possemen or perhaps cattlemen. He was doing everything about this possibility but wringing his hands, which he could not do very successfully since he had horse-reins in them. But he lamented and eventually the pair of stoic individuals on the wagon began to steadily regard him. If something were repeated often enough, whether folks actually began believing it or not, it certainly had its effect upon them.

Smoke spat down the side of the wagon and Douglas sat up there looking as though he were a real Indian wearing a real turban. Nat was at the highest point of his lamentations when Douglas said, "You want to bet a silver dollar?"

That stopped Nat. He did not gamble very often because he could not stand to lose.

Douglas held up a cartwheel. "Dollar we see her soon. You bet a dollar we don't see her soon."

Nat got cautious. "What is 'soon'? You mean in the next hour or the next ten minutes?"

Smoke showed disgust with his partner. "Bet him or shut up," he growled at Nat.

Douglas continued to hold up the silver coin. Nat considered the dollar, the face of McTavish, the look he was getting from his partner, then he turned to ride alongside the wagon, hands clasped atop the saddlehorn looking intently all around.

He saw her, finally, sitting on the middle slope of a piny-woods slope northwest of them a short distance, upon the left-hand side of the road. He swore with feeling and turned accusingly, but Douglas had already put away his silver dollar.

"Tried to trick me," Nat complained. "He'd seen her and tried to trick me into betting."

Smoke agreed. "Yeah. And he'd have succeeded if you hadn't been such a chicken-liver," Smoke looked out where the girl was watching them, looking dead ahead on up the road in the direction of a stone trough at the rear sector of a large turn-out, and whistled to make the mules pick up their gait a little. He then waved a hand high overhead and gestured for the girl to ride on over and meet them at the turn-out.

She did not move. Smoke lowered his arm with a sigh. He had forgotten how wary she was.

Nathan got up to the turn-out first, stepped down and loosened the cincha, removed the headstall and bit so his horse could drink at the trough, then he hobbled the animal and after draping the bridle from the horn, turned to guide Smoke on in. No matter how large the turn-outs were along mountain roads, they were almost never wide enough nor deep enough to accommodate a vehicle any larger than a stagecoach—for which most of them had been created.

But Smoke Lunceford was one of those rare drivers who could herd his hitch as though it were much smaller and was attached to a light buggy. He cut the corner just right and allowing for wheel-drift to the point of perfection sidled the wagon off the coachroad until it was parked levelly, and athwart the turn-off. It was a masterful job of driving, of parking, and of knowing the exact temperament of his hitch in order to get each animal to cooperate so well.

Nathan did not comment but Douglas looked admiringly at Lunceford.

The girl was nowhere in sight as Smoke climbed down. He let down the tailgate so that Douglas could climb out if he chose to, then he turned slowly to scan each rock and tree close by and still did not see her.

Nat came round back for the buckets to water the hitch with. He winked at Douglas, shoved two bucket-bales into his partner's hands and jerked his head to indicate that Smoke should come along.

The sky was flawless up here, the air was not entirely warm yet which meant that it still had the faint aroma of wild flowers and pine-sap in it.

There were jaunty little blue-gray tree-squirrels with great bushy tails and little upright pointed ears, watching everything the men did. There were also birds of innumerable species close by. Evidently this turn-out with its trough of spring-water was the focal point of a lot of different kinds of lives.

Nat lugged water, tanked up mules, went back empty and refilled the buckets and lugged them back again, acting as immersed in his work as he usually acted, but when he and Smoke happened to be at the trough together, one time, he leaned and said, "Off to your left back through the trees just west of the tailgate—and don't gawk." Then Nat refilled his buckets and headed briskly back to water more mules.

Smoke saw the girl, finally. She was on foot and if she had her gun he could detect no sign of it. She had her hair loose instead of braided, and she was erect and lithe and handsome where she stood watching the wagon.

She was fair with jet-shaded hair and eyes, and although she was not as tall as many Sioux women were, she was handsomely rounded.

Smoke sighed, spat, turned reluctantly back to refill the buckets, and then turned fully to go over and water mules. He watched around the side of the long head of a drinking mule, from the corner of his eye. She did not come closer, but when she moved a little, evidently to attract someone's attention—not Smoke's attention and not Nat's attention—Douglas straightened up off the tailgate. He too had seen her.

Nat edged in close to his partner to say, "I figure she's putting him in a hell of a spot. She expects him to go off with her through the forest."

"Well; what's wrong with that?"

"He'll figure he owes us. You'll see."

They continued to haul water. A mule could drink more than someone thought, who had never tried to fill one up, a bucketload at a time. Finally, when the last team raised dripping muzzles, and looked around, Smoke set down the buckets and turned fully in the direction of the girl.

She was not there.

He looked left and right, decided she must have slipped over to the tailgate after all, despite her dread of white-men, and leaned to retrieve the buckets, to offer the last of the water to the tanked-up mules. They refused it.

Nat was at the trough, buckets at his feet, leaning over there making a cigarette. As Smoke strode over Nat looked steadily at him, then he twisted the paper, popped the quirley between his lips and felt round for a match to strike upon the stonework he was propped against.

"They are both gone," he told Smoke, and did not sound as though this pleased him, for some reason. "I'd have bet new money Douglas would have come along and thanked us first."

Smoke was unconcerned. "You don't have to thank folks. They know you're grateful to them. Anyway, whatever we did for him we didn't do for his thanks nor his gratitude."

From behind them up the slope overlooking the stone trough McTavish called down to them. "I got to leave you now." They turned and Smoke said, "You're in no shape to go anywhere. You heard what that pill-roller said. You got to lie low and do nothing for a couple more weeks."

Douglas smiled at Smoke. "I know. That's what I'm going to do. She'll look after me. You fellers . . . I'll never forget either of you."

Nat grunted. "Humph! You keep an eye on that girl, Douglas. If she gets mad at you, look out. Grab her wrists otherwise she'll darn near scalp you with just her fingernails. You mind her now, you understand?"

McTavish considered Nat a moment before widely smiling at him. "She says about the same thing about you. If you ever get a woman, she says someone had ought to warn her you are strong as a bull."

Nat smiled. "Rest a lot and move slow, and keep to the mountains until all the ruckus dies down. Good luck, Douglas."

McTavish raised a hand, palm forward, and while he was still smiling he turned and moved back to be swallowed immediately by fragrant forest shadows. Smoke and Nathan did not catch a sighting of the girl.

Smoke spat, leaned to rinse his mouth at the trough, straightened up and looked ahead up the pass where sunshine was just now beginning to show in all its full golden splendor. "Well, hell," he exclaimed, "standing around here isn't goin' to put us midway down the far side by evening, is it?"

They had to raise the tailgate and chain it into place, then Nat got astride his horse, Smoke climbed back to the high seat, and they struck out up through the slot of mountain pass which was lined on both sides by forest giants so thick and tall there was nothing but perpetual gloom back out through on both sides as far as a man could see.

They were two miles further along with the top-out well in sight, which meant the worst part of their uphill haul was over, when Nat reined in upon the left side of the wagon, close, and looking upwards, said, "You ever wonder what'd happen if you found one that pretty, who didn't fight you like a catamount and didn't run off like a deer every time you looked at her?"

Smoke smiled while looking ahead up through the high ears of his mules. "Yeah; I've thought of it a few times."

"What did you come up with?"

He looked down at Nat. "I'm still driving this wagon, ain't I?"

Nathan turned that over in his mind, and meanwhile they got up to the top-out where the roadway ran as level as a tabletop for about a mile. The mules eased up in their collar-pads. Shortly now the freighters would halt, would get out their binder-chains and fix the rear-wheel skids which were commonly employed on a long down-grade, even when the wagon was not fully laden.

Good teamsters, like good stockmen of any other kind, favored their animals every chance they got.

Nathan pointed where a big white rock stood at the side of the road. "Stop up there, eh?"

Smoke obeyed without commenting, then he climbed down to join his partner in rigging up the wheel-skids, and while he was on his back beneath the big old wagon, he said, "You ever think what'd happen if you caught one, and she didn't try to tear out your hair?"

Nathan had. "Quite a few times, to tell you the fact of it. Trouble is . . . I never been able to make up my mind what I'd do."

"You'd rather go shagging-butt all over creation beside this big old wagon, than make a decent cabin beside a lake somewhere and just settle in?"

"I got to tell you honestly, I don't know, Smoke."

"Take the tag-end of the chain over through the opposite wheel now . . . And you are crazy. You got to be crazy to even have to think about it."

"By gawd, you're still with the wagon!"

157

Smoke struggled upright once he had wiggled from beneath the rig. "Sure, and I never said *I* wasn't crazy . . . Twist that darned chain tighter'n that or the wheel will chatter all the way down."

"Who the hell you ordering around? I've set as many of these skids as you have!"

Smoke dusted off as best he could after having been on the ground under the wagon, then he walked around to look at his partner's handiwork on the other side.

He said, "On second thought you'd better stay with the wagon, too. You got a lousy disposition. You'd make a poor husband, but you make a pretty fair freighter." Smoke stepped past and started up the side of the wagon to the high seat. Nathan stood down there watching, until Smoke was evening up the lines, then Nat shook his head and went over to swing up astride his saddlehorse.

They started across the rim to the far side, and went down two miles with the skid working perfectly before they found a turn-out which was adequate for the camp, and down there as they were readying the mules for their hobbled and limited freedom, Nathan said, "Yeah, I think you're right."

Smoke scowled. "About what?"

"About me not having the disposition for a husband . . . Did you move that bottle of whisky?"

"Nope, you old granny, it's still wrapped in the sack beneath the seat."

They exchanged a look, laughed, and Nathan went over to rummage under the wagon-seat.

The sun was still an hour-high when they gathered faggots for their supper fire, and mixed creek-water in their tin cups with the whisky. There were fifteen miles of mighty mountains between them and what they'd got embroiled with southward. As far as they were both concerned, that entire interlude was finished. Tomorrow was another day, this side of the mountains was new territory, and they had that bottle of whisky to help them digest their supper and to afterwards sit around in reverie until it was time to sleep. Maybe their life wasn't the easiest in the world, but neither was it the worst.

Center Point Publishing
600 Brooks Road ● PO Box 1
Thorndike ME 04986-0001 USA

(207) 568-3717

**US & Canada:
1 800 929-9108**
www.centerpointlargeprint.com